THE MARK TWAIN MURDERS

Also by Laurence Yep

SWEETWATER

DRAGONWINGS

CHILD OF THE OWL

SEA GLASS

· LAURENCE YEP ·

THE MARK TWAIN MURDERS

Four Winds Press   New York

LIBRARY OF CONGRESS CATALOGING IN PUBLICATION DATA

Yep, Laurence.
  The Mark Twain murders.

  Summary: In the summer of 1864, a teen-age boy meets
reporter Mark Twain in San Francisco after a murder,
and agrees to help him get the story.
  1. Twain, Mark, 1835-1910—Juvenile fiction.
[1. Twain, Mark, 1835-1910—Fiction. 2. Mystery and
detective stories. 3. San Francisco (Calif.)—Fiction]
I. Title.
PZ7.Y44Mar   [Fic]   81-69510
ISBN 0-590-07824-0   AACR2

PUBLISHED BY FOUR WINDS PRESS

A DIVISION OF SCHOLASTIC INC., NEW YORK, N.Y.

COPYRIGHT © 1982 BY LAURENCE YEP

ALL RIGHTS RESERVED

PRINTED IN THE UNITED STATES OF AMERICA

LIBRARY OF CONGRESS CATALOG CARD NUMBER: 81-69510

1 2 3 4 5 86 85 84 83 82

To Michael and Shira,
who were there when it began.

PROLOGUE

Before Mark Twain wrote *Tom Sawyer* and *Huckleberry Finn*, in fact, before he wrote "The Celebrated Jumping Frog of Calaveras County," which first gained national recognition for him, he was a reporter for a San Francisco newspaper. This story is set during the summer of 1864. While the story itself is fiction, it is based upon actual events of that time.

· CHAPTER ·

1

In San Francisco nowadays, you can find an awful lot of folks who will claim that they knew Mark Twain when he was just starting out as a reporter for the newspapers. To hear them tell it, they were always at his side, sharpening his pencils and patting him on the shoulder and telling him what a great writer he was. Well, sir, I just sit and laugh at those folks because I know the truth: Back then, Mark was about as welcome as a skunk at a Sunday picnic.

The first time I ever laid eyes on him was back during the Civil War and I didn't think very much of what I saw. All the other reporters were busy twisting their heads this way and that like vultures and scribbling away in their notebooks. But Mark just stood in the hallway outside the bedroom, his face all pasty white, staring straight ahead. I don't think he liked the look and smell of murder.

The corpse lay under an old blanket in the very center of the small, crowded room. I watched as the police detective, the celebrated Bulldog Brill himself, walked toward the body. Bulldog had gotten his name because he had the heavy jowls of a bulldog and a soul to match.

It was said that once Bulldog smelled an evildoer's trail, he didn't stop until he had sunk his teeth into the criminal's leg. Only he looked kind of tired right then— like an overworked watchdog.

He picked up one corner of the blanket and nodded his head to me. "Is this your father, young Dougherty?"

It was definitely the man who had called himself my father. I looked at the corpse and recognized the angry, twisted face. There was a small triangular hole in the center of his throat; identical holes and spots covered his body. And, as the dime novels will tell you, he was lying in a pool of his own blood which was slowly darkening from red to brown.

The sight took most of the starch out of me. I tried to talk and found my voice had slipped away. I gave a cough and managed a hoarse whisper. "That's Johnny Dougherty, all right," I said, "but he wasn't my father."

Bulldog Brill looked at me sharply. "Who was he, then?"

"My stepfather." I took off my top hat. The silk was torn on the side, and it had been pretty much battered out of shape before I had found it on the trash heap. "My real father," I announced with all the dignity I could muster, "was an English lord." I set my hat back on my head with a jaunty tap to the crown. "And I am His Grace, the Duke of Baywater."

I could hear the laughter behind me from the reporters; but before I could say anything, a sandy-haired corporal wriggled his way from the hallway into the room. His index finger made a circular motion by his temple. "Johnny used to tell me how crazy he was."

Bulldog dropped the blanket to cover the corpse

again. "And who might you be?"

"Malloy, sir." The corporal saluted smartly. "Corporal Aloysius Malloy of the army of this grand country of the United States of America." He pronounced each syllable of his name with relish. "You see, Johnny made the mistake of marrying a woman from one of those ritzy families, and she filled the boy's head with so many notions that"—he shrugged—"that he got the idea he actually had a duke for a father."

I squared my shoulders, having learned how to handle people like Malloy. "And I'm telling you that Johnny Dougherty behaved like no natural father. He was always beating my mother, and when she died, he started in on me until I ran away a year ago. The only reason he ever looked for me after that was to take whatever I had in my pockets."

Bulldog stuck out his jaw. "If beatings are all you need to be a lost lord, then half of San Francisco could be nobility," he growled. "Let's stick to facts." Taking out a notebook, he glanced at a page before he nodded to the corporal. "Dougherty was in your squad at the Black Point Military Reservation, wasn't he?"

"That he was, your honor." Malloy dipped his head nervously, as if eager to please. "And until he deserted last night, I thought he was going to shape up into a good soldier."

"Why do you think he left?" Bulldog demanded.

Malloy tugged unhappily at the visor of his cap. "Well, he was real good friends with a fellow called Billy Gogarty. Then, two nights ago, Billy deserted. I think Johnny must have gone looking for him."

Bulldog frowned at Malloy. "Those wounds look like

they were made by a bayonet. Are you missing one?"

Malloy looked embarrassed. "It's possible. We haven't held an inspection yet."

Bulldog sighed. "No wonder we can't win this war— we've got an army that can't keep track of its soldiers *or* its weapons." He studied his notebook and then looked back at Malloy. "The landlady says a big fellow checked in here two nights ago."

"Billy Gogarty is big." The corporal snatched off his cap melodramatically. "He must have done the foul deed."

Before she died, my mother had tried to teach me a number of things that a gentleman ought to know and do; and one thing a gentleman did was to stick up for the truth. "Billy Gogarty might be a big man," I spoke up strong and true, "but he's as simple as they come. And besides, he doesn't have a mean bone in his body."

Malloy seemed glad of being able to shout at someone else for a change instead of being shouted at. "And how would you be knowing that?"

Bulldog tapped Malloy on the arm. "Hey, you talk to me, not to the little lord."

"I'm sorry, your honor, but the boy and his fancy airs kind of got to me." Malloy shot a poisonous glance at me and then faced Bulldog again. "All right now, I admit that Billy was simple just like the boy said and nice enough when he and Johnny joined up two months ago." Malloy shrugged. "But last week he somehow got the idea we wanted to hang him. I guess he finally got so scared that he ran away."

A chubby, pear-shaped soldier pushed into the room right then. He had looked familiar when I saw him out in the hallway; but I hadn't been able to tag him with a name until now. He was Felix Pettibone—one of Johnny Dougherty's cutthroat friends.

"Johnny was just trying to talk Billy into coming back." Every ounce of Felix's smile was weighted and measured for effect. "Johnny didn't want him to get into any serious trouble."

The others might not have had the measure of the man, but I did. "And butter wouldn't melt in your mouth, would it, Felix?" I pointed down at the corpse. "If Billy actually killed Johnny Dougherty, then you can bet Johnny must have given him good cause."

For all the fat on Felix, there was still a good deal of muscle. When he hit me on the side of the head, I spun around once and fell to my hands and knees right by the bed.

"Now that's enough of that," Bulldog snarled to Felix. "Are you all right, boy?" Bulldog stood over me protectively.

I rubbed my head. "I think so." As I started to get to my feet, I caught a glimpse of something under the bed. It looked like a coin. It was too large to be a dime, and yet when I picked it up it felt too thin and light to be a penny. Puzzled, I handed it to Bulldog. "Do you know what this is?"

Bulldog weighed the coin in his hand. "This must be one of those new brass pennies." He held it up by the edge so he could examine it better.

I leaned forward to inspect it, too. "So that's what they look like." Because of a shortage of metals caused by the war, the U.S. government had given up using copper and nickel in its pennies and switched to a different formula.

Bulldog flipped the coin back to me. I caught it in

midair. "Here, Your Grace. Keep it. It might change your luck."

"That's *my* lucky penny." Felix came over. His smile was gone now. "Johnny borrowed it from me to show to some of the boys. He just forgot to give it back. It must have fallen out of his pocket during the fight with Billy."

"So you say." I tucked the penny away safely in my pants pocket. "But I don't see your name on it."

Felix grated his words out harshly. "I want what's mine."

I kept my hand in my pocket. "You mean you want anything that isn't nailed down." I jerked my head at Felix. "It's an old trick of yours to claim any lost item."

Bulldog collared Felix and dragged him back a few steps. "Say, just where were you last night, soldier boy?"

"I was in the guardhouse." Felix pointed at me. "And as sure as there are harps in heaven, that's my penny."

Bulldog nodded his head for me to go. "You'd better leave. I've got enough to do without having to stop people from hitting you."

"This way, lad." A policeman took me gently but firmly by the arm and steered me through the crowd out into the hallway of that dingy rooming house. I was just heading down the stairs leading to the front door when I heard a voice call out, "Hold on there."

I turned around to see that it was the odd reporter who hadn't written down anything. I can't say I was very impressed when I had a chance to study him better. His head seemed too big for his body and his thick, curly red hair and long sideburns made his head seem even wider than it really was.

He was clean shaven and wore a kind of wide silk tie

called a cravat tied under his high wing collar and a top hat of expensive plush beaver. All in all, though, he looked just like some boy who was trying to dress like a rich silver baron.

I just kept right on going. The stories my mother had told me had never covered this situation, but I was sure that a proper gentleman did not associate with reporters.

He was a little out of breath when he caught up to me. "That Pettibone is mighty rough company." He had a slow, lazy way of talking.

"All of Johnny's friends were pretty rough," I said, and watched contemptuously as he took out a notebook and pencil. Now that he was out of sight of the corpse, he seemed to have remembered he was a reporter again.

"What about Billy Gogarty?" he asked.

"Billy was simply the muscle they used for breaking down doors and for carrying away the loot." I gave a sad laugh. "The joke was that he thought they were his friends because they bought him beers and let him sleep on their floors. Inside, he was a kind, gentle man."

"I don't know about the gentleness," he said, "but Gogarty certainly seemed kind enough at sharing his bayonet." He flipped open his notebook. "I'm not partial to such charity myself."

"You didn't know Johnny Dougherty and you don't know his friends." The wind was blowing the dust around the way it usually did in San Francisco, and I rubbed my eyes. "This Australian by the name of Digger used Johnny and Billy in a lot of his schemes. My guess is that Digger got them into something so big that Billy got scared and wanted out." I made a slashing motion across my throat. "So Digger ordered Johnny to kill

Billy—only Billy made a sieve out of Johnny instead."

The reporter eagerly scratched something in his note-book. "So you really think that Gogarty might have killed Dougherty in self-defense?"

I leaned my head back to look at him carefully. "My time doesn't come free, you know."

His eyes narrowed. "You're awfully young to be saying things like that. How old are you? Thirteen?"

"Fifteen." I swept my top hat off and bowed to him as my mother had taught me. "I'm small for my age."

He chewed the end of his pencil. "That's still mighty young to be so cold-blooded."

I carefully polished a spot on the brim of my top hat. "My mother trained me for a better way of life than the one I'm leading right now. I intend to reach my proper station some day; and I won't make it if I give stories away for free." I pulled my hat down carefully over my head. "Besides, I can get you inside information that no one else has."

Mark frowned. "What sort of information?"

"I know a place where Billy used to go all the time." I was careful just to give him enough information to whet his appetite. "You can write about him from an angle that no one else will have." I added, "But it's going to cost you."

"What's this world coming to?" Mournfully he tugged at his sideburns. Finally he came to a decision. "All right. I'll pay you a dollar."

"Real money?" I asked cautiously. To pay for the war, President Lincoln had taken to printing paper dollars that no one wanted. In fact, a dollar "greenback" was only worth thirty-five cents in coins.

"I'll use true silver." He held up a hand. "I swear."

"That's your left hand," I pointed out. "I'll want half the money now and half when we're finished." I held out my palm.

He dug around in his pockets and then gave a miserable little cough. "Well, I'll have to pay you tomorrow. That's payday."

"In that case, forget it." I started to walk away.

"Tell you what. Help me now and I'll pay you *two* dollars tomorrow." He raised his hand. "I promise."

"That's your left hand again." I felt obliged to tell him.

"I forgot." Sheepishly he held up his right hand. "I swear on my sainted mother's grave that I'll pay you the money on Saturday."

"Is your mother dead?" I didn't trust him much.

"My grandmother's then, dang it." He thrust his head forward defiantly. "She's both dead *and* sainted if Heaven goes by a voice vote in her town. So what do you say?"

I told him the honest truth. "You'd promise me the moon if you could get your story; but when it came time to collect, it'd be another matter."

He blinked his eyes once. "Look. Help me now and you can stick tighter than my own shadow until I pay you back."

I thought about it for a while. "All right. It's a deal, Mister? . . ."

"Twain. Mark Twain. Of the *Daily Morning Call*."

My jaw dropped. "Not *the* Mark Twain, from Nevada."

"You've read my stories?" He preened himself self-consciously by tugging at his vest.

"I've met a lot of men who've been chased out of one town or another, but this is the first time I've ever met a man who was chased out of an entire state—and Nevada at that."

"Y-a-a-s, well," he mumbled, "I suppose that is some sort of distinction."

"That isn't the word I would have used." I held the lapels of my coat in my hands. "*Why* did you write those hoaxes?"

Mark Twain winced like I'd just hit him in the stomach. When he spoke, it was in a tired, embarrassed way as if he had given the same explanation a hundred times. "Hoaxes are part of the newspaper business there. It's part of frontier humor to see if you can sell someone on a story." He added defensively, "I always left plenty of clues in the articles so the careful reader would know the stories were fake."

"I heard you wrote a story about an Indian who got so lost in thought he hardened into stone hundreds of years ago."

"That was my first." Mark Twain gave a little chuckle. "But you know the other western newspapers printed it as the gospel turth?" He scratched the back of his head. "I'm afraid my imagination soared even higher after that."

"There's some folks who say your imagination soared too often and too far." After a number of other hoaxes, Mark Twain had written an article claiming that the good ladies of Nevada had misused money raised for a charity. People in Nevada had gotten so angry that someone had actually challenged Twain to a pistol duel. To save his skin, he had left Nevada on a fast stagecoach.

"Y-a-a-s, well," he drawled, "you're now looking at a reformed man. Nowadays I tell a truth so strong that I have to water it down for most folks."

"In that case, I'll help you." I spat into my hand and held it out. With a grin, Twain spat into his own before he shook hands with me solemnly.

Then we started to make our way around the hill—which sounds a lot easier than it actually was. You didn't so much walk through San Francisco as you worked your way across it. You see, San Francisco had become a city only some fifteen years before, when the gold rush started. Most of the streets weren't paved yet but only had planks laid over them; and time and hard use had worn large holes in a lot of the planks.

The sidewalks, which were also made from planks, were not much better, since the streets and houses followed the rolling contours of the ground. The streets were likely to tilt first to the left and then to the right and at the same time to dip and rise like the backs of snakes squirming their separate ways across the city.

Adding to the mess were all the different construction projects. The city had only recently adopted uniform grades for the streets so that entire blocks were being torn up, smoothed out, and replanked. Some houses had to be raised up to the new level of the street while others had to have stairs built from their front doors to the new street level which might be as much as ten feet below. A number of people had simply moved their houses to flatter land.

Mark Twain kept talking all the while. He told me all about his life—from the time he grew up in Missouri to the time when he became a riverboat pilot and then his try at finding a silver mine in Nevada before he took on a job writing for a Nevada newspaper. It wasn't always his fault, I suppose, but it sounded like the man had failed at everything he tried. At the age of twenty-eight, he was trying to make a fresh start.

When we finally circled around to the south slope of Telegraph Hill, we both paused—not only to catch our breath but to take in the view as well. San Francisco was not all that big a city then. Beginning from where we stood, the city covered only some ten square miles.

Just below us a few small frame houses clung to the top of the hill with picket fences and small gardens identical to those of the houses on the windward side of the hill. However, as the sides of the hill plunged toward more level ground, the houses began to jam together tightly side by side, their fronts crowding right up against the sidewalk with no room for gardens or yards. A sea of shingled roofs and church spires seemed to flow from the foot of the hill toward the bay and the ships with their masts and smokestacks. On this side of the hill, life usually moved a little quicker and hearts beat just a little faster.

"The whole city smells of raw lumber and new paint." Mark half turned and sniffed at the air. "Just as if it was slapped together overnight."

"I guess it was in a way," I said. The rich men might own the houses, but anybody could own the view. "It's already been burnt to the ground and rebuilt a few times."

On the eastern slopes of Telegraph Hill stood the saloons and sporting houses of the area that was becoming known as the Barbary Coast. I could just make out the gleaming rock walls exposed by a street-widening project. Blasting and hammering had been going on for a week on Broadway Street, but there was an ominous silence at the project now. To our right lay Fern Hill† with the houses scattered loosely on its steep, sandy slopes. Excavations had only recently begun to connect the streets on either side of its summit. Tracks were being laid on the western side of the hill so that cars could carry the sand to fill in the depressions on Larkin Street, the western boundary of the city.

I pointed beyond the hills across the broad expanse of Market Street, toward the elegant brownstone mansions and lawns at the foot and top of Rincon Hill. "That's where I'm going to live some day."

"Of course you are." Twain was doing his best to control a smile.

"You think it's a joke, don't you?" I lowered my arm. "Well, let me tell you something, Mr. Twain. If you don't take yourself seriously, then nobody will." And I started down the hill.

†Fern Hill later became known as Nob Hill, when cable cars made its slopes accessible to the rich who were nicknamed "nobs."

· CHAPTER ·
2

When we reached Vallejo Street, Twain took off his hat. "Say, just where are we going?"

I pointed at the white spire of a church. "To Father Keegan's. Billy likcd to visit him so they could talk."

Twain scratched his cheek. "I thought priests had something that wouldn't let them talk about confessions."

I held up a hand. "Don't worry, you'll get your money's worth. If Father Keegan can't help you, I'll take you to Digger."

But when we got to the church, we found it was still locked up tight from the night before, so we went to the rectory next door where Father Keegan lived. On the rectory door was a neatly printed sign:

> **I am terribly sorry but I am feeling too sick to hold morning Mass today.**
>
> **Rev. Keegan**

"That's funny." I scratched my forehead. "I wonder why Father Keegan didn't get a replacement."

Twain leaned his hand against the door. "Especially

today." He rubbed his chin. "Lincoln's declared today a day of public prayer. We're all supposed to ask for an end to the war."

No one answered when I used the door knocker. I knocked again, but there was still no answer. I started to knock a third time when the door opened and a man with pockmarked cheeks said, "I'm sick."

Father Keegan did look pretty pale and tired to me, as if he had been up all night, but his eyes were wide open—more like he was sick with fear rather than fever. "Sorry to bother you, Father." I began to back toward the street. "Our mistake."

Suddenly the priest disappeared, and in his place was a heavy-set giant dressed in black pants and a blue sailor's coat. His ears were swollen as if he'd been in too many fights. In his right hand was a bayonet with rust-brown stains along its length. "I thought I heard your voice, Duke."

"Aye, Billy, it's me." I stood my ground, but I didn't feel too good looking at the bloody bayonet.

"And who's this?" Billy's eyes narrowed suspiciously, and he pointed at Twain with the bayonet.

Twain looked as if he wanted to run, but somehow his feet had not gotten the message. The only thing Twain could move was his left arm. With it, he lifted his hat. "Howdy."

Billy closed a giant paw over Twain's shoulder and jerked him inside the rectory. Then Billy tossed me on top of Twain as he lay sprawled on the hallway floor.

I scrambled to my feet, afraid that Billy might hurt the reporter. "Billy"—I tried to sound stern, but my voice cracked from fear—"that's no way to treat a friend of mine. That's an important man. He's Mark Twain of the *Call*."

Billy slammed the door shut and shot the bolt home. "I don't like reporters."

"The feeling is mutual." Twain sat up, dusting off his coat sleeves.

As scared as I was at that moment, I actually felt sorry for Billy. Of all Johnny's friends, I had always gotten along best with him. It was easy to trick Billy—too easy, so I never took him for more than a penny or two. But Johnny or Felix or another of his so-called friends would cheat him out of everything he had in his pockets. Billy knew he could relax and be friendly with me and still come away with most of his money.

"Billy," I said, "you can't stay here. The police are going to come by to ask Father Keegan questions, just like we did."

The little priest adjusted the spectacles on his nose. "Isn't that just what I've been telling you, Billy?"

Billy stared at a wall as if in a daze, his free hand mechanically massaging his throat. "They'll hang me."

Father Keegan helped Twain to his feet. "Not if you tell them what you've told me."

"Tell them what?" I prompted Billy. "You trust me, don't you?"

Billy's lips parted moistly, his eyes widening. He stared at the bayonet in his other hand. "Johnny . . . Johnny was going to kill me." He closed his free hand into a hamlike fist and punched at the air. "I fought him." He paused and held both hands to reveal the scabs on their backs. "See? And then I . . . then I. . . ." He suddenly raised his right arm above his head and I cringed, ducking my head. "I reaches up and I grabs the bayonet from his hand. I grabs it"—his fingers readjusted their grip on the bayonet's lower end—"and I stabs out. Johnny screams. I hold on. I want him to stop. I keep on stabbing." Billy thrust at the air repeatedly with the bayonet. "I keep on stabbing until he stops."

"We'll tell them that, Billy," Father Keegan said soothingly.

"That's right," I chimed in eagerly. "It was self-defense, pure and simple."

Billy shook his head slowly as if in a dream. "You don't understand. Johnny was always telling me that I gotta be quiet, or I'd wind up dead." Billy gazed straight ahead and swallowed. "It's not so much dying that I mind. A bullet or a knife, they're quick. But there's something about the thought of hanging . . . I mean, they say . . . they say you can't control yourself, you know." Billy raised one shoulder, embarrassed. He wouldn't look at me.

Fear in a man as large as Billy seemed a sad sight to me. Despite his size, he was basically no more violent than a small bird.

Suddenly there was a loud knock at the door. Billy lifted the bayonet threateningly. After a few moments, someone knocked again. "This is the police," a man announced. "We'd like to talk to you, Father."

The four of us froze for a moment in the hallway. Billy's eyes started darting all around as if he were trying to find a hole into which he could crawl. I had seen that same look in rats down on the wharves when they were trapped. It was easy for them to panic then and hurt someone. If that was the case, Billy was just as likely to use that bayonet on one of us.

But both Father Keegan and Twain didn't seem to know what to do, so I took the lead. "Billy," I tried to say, but it came out only as a croak. I swallowed and tried again. This time my voice was much firmer. "It's all over now. Give yourself up before you get shot."

"Shot?" Billy frowned at the bayonet in his hand.

He was not really anything more than a big overgrown boy and I treated him like that. "Drop the bayonet," I scolded him in the same gentle but firm voice my mother once used.

Billy leaned back against the wall. "But, Duke, I told you why I can't."

"Billy"—I made my voice sterner—"I've had enough. Give me the bayonet."

"Father?" The policeman sounded more impatient now. "We really have to talk to you."

Billy rolled his eyes for a moment toward the door. His fist tightened around the bayonet.

"Billy, no." I put my hand on his wrist.

He jerked back as if my hand was on fire and, with one great sweep of his free hand, sent me flying backward against Twain and Father Keegan with such force that the three of us collapsed into a clutter of arms and legs.

"You're just making things worse," Father Keegan called from the bottom of the heap. "Don't run away."

But Billy was already lumbering past us down the hallway. By the time I disentangled myself from the others, Billy was running out the back door.

"Father, what's wrong?" the policeman called anxiously.

"Don't shoot. I'm coming." Father Keegan hurried

past me to unbolt and open the front door. "Billy went out the back way," he said to the policeman.

The officer turned to his partner. "Jerry, see what you can do about heading him off." Then he was dashing past us with a pistol in one hand and a nightstick in the other.

Twain watched the officer disappear out the back door and then picked up his hat where he had dropped it in the hallway. "You handled Gogarty real well." He sounded surprised.

I tried to shrug it off. "Billy isn't really a killer."

Twain brushed his hat off with his sleeve. "Y-a-a-s, well, I suppose it might just have been self-defense after all. But we're probably the only people in San Francisco who think that."

Billy got away. We had to go over to make our statements at the police station in the basement of the city hall. When we were finished, Mark smiled at Bulldog. "How about letting me look at your report on Gogarty?"

"Since when did ignorance stop you from writing?" Bulldog shuffled the papers in his hands.

"Bulldog," Twain said quietly, "I really do need the help. My editor's been after me to tighten up my stories." Twain held up his hand. "I swear this is the last time I'll ask you for a favor."

Bulldog picked up a file and weighed it in his hand thoughtfully. "That's what you said when you borrowed that twenty dollars from me two weeks ago." He slowly fanned himself with the file. "Detectives don't make that much, you know. Not the honest ones, anyway."

Twain put up both hands this time. "This coming payday," he promised. I glanced at Twain. It seemed to me that the contents of his pay envelope was going to be stretched pretty thin; but he did not even bat an eyelash when he added, "I swear by the Almighty that you'll get your money then."

Bulldog sat back in his chair in mock alarm. "I wish you wouldn't swear when I'm sitting so close to you, Mark. A fellow could get hit by lightning."

"I've taken the oath before and ain't been hit yet, Bulldog." Twain snatched the file from his hand.

"Then heaven must be sorely tempted by now." Bulldog rummaged around in the stack of files, pulling out several more. "Well, I suppose I'd better protect my investment. Here's some more cases for you. There was a burglary at a bookstore, a shoplifting case, and some other things." He piled them in Twain's lap.

Twain took down the information in the other files first before he turned to Billy's. When he was finished, he lowered the report. "Is this all?"

Bulldog threw his pen into his ink bottle. "Just how many murders does your newspaper want? And anyway, that's only a preliminary file with notes on my interrogation and some details of the search."

Twain took the stack of reports and set them on one of the smaller piles on the detective's desk. "You know what I mean, Bulldog. You've got it sounding like murder."

Bulldog blew on the sheet of paper in front of him and then began to blot it carefully. "Billy admits killing Johnny Dougherty."

"Sane people don't carry around a bloody bayonet.

And anyway, he says it was self-defense." Twain crossed his legs and settled back. "You heard young Baywater here tell about Johnny Dougherty and Gogarty."

Bulldog lifted the blotter carefully. "We not only have the corpse, we know who the murderer is, and that's a hundred percent more than we usually have." He nodded his head toward a filing cabinet four drawers high. "See that cabinet? Each drawer is full of unsolved murders. I'll be happy if we can actually catch the killer."

"Bulldog"—Twain stared steadily at his friend—"you ought to check out the boy's story at least."

Bulldog put a fresh sheet of paper down in front of himself. "All right, what sort of plot was Gogarty tied up in?" He lifted his pen.

"I don't know the details," I said, "but if you talk to Digger. . . ." My words trailed off as Bulldog laid his pen down.

"What's the matter, Bulldog?" Twain asked.

Bulldog stared at both of us, tapping his fingers upon the desk top. "Mark, your faith in me is touching, but I've got a file full of warrants for Digger."

"Well, why don't you go get him?" Twain snapped.

"It would take at least a dozen police to find him and bring him here." Bulldog leaned back, clasping one hand at the back of his head. "He's a mean double-dealer from the fifties. Used to be a shanghaier." The detective actually chuckled. "One time he announced he was retiring, so he invited all of his friends. . . ."

"I wouldn't think the man would have many friends." Twain tucked his notebook safely away in his pocket.

"Fellow professionals, then," Bulldog nodded. "Anyway, he had them all get on this tug and took them out for a party on the bay. Well, they got to drinking and whooping it up for about an hour, and then everyone but Digger and the tugboat captain drops down asleep." He slapped his hand against his thigh. "He'd shanghaied the whole lot of them." He shook his head. "For a whole year, the ships had to deal exclusively with Digger because he'd shipped all his rivals off to the four corners of the world." He cocked his head to one side. "They say he smuggles guns now to the Juaristas in Mexico."

Twain leaned forward excitedly. "Maybe this Digger fellow got Gogarty and the others into a gun-smuggling plot."

Bulldog smiled with one corner of his mouth, skeptically. "Even if that wild story was true, Mark, what makes you think I could get anything out of Digger?" He picked up a new file. "Now get out. I've got better things to do than to nursemaid the laziest reporter in all of San Francisco."

"Now hold on," Twain protested. "I'm the only local reporter on the *Call* when they need two."

"Plenty of newspapers make do with only one reporter, and you know it." Bulldog sounded almost bored as he began reading through the file. "Face the facts, Mark. You just don't have it."

I waited until we were outside the police station before I asked Twain, "Why didn't you tell off that detective? Don't you have any pride at all? I'd never let anyone call me lazy."

"I was afraid," he said calmly, "that Bulldog would reach into one of his many filing cabinets and drag out the proof for what he said."

My opinion of Mr. Mark Twain went real low right

then. I'd never known anyone so down on their luck that they didn't at least have the backbone to stand up for their own good name. "If you don't respect yourself, how do you expect others to respect you?"

"Not everyone's an English lord," he snapped.

When he turned southward toward Kearney Street, I plucked at his sleeve. "That isn't the way to Digger's."

Twain shoved my hand away. "I already risked my neck once today. Didn't you hear what Bulldog just said about Digger? He sounds twice as dangerous as a pit full of rattlesnakes."

"We don't have to talk to Digger." I wrinkled my nose. "We can just sniff around."

"Maybe some other day." He glanced up at the sun. "It's getting late, and I can't spare the time." He held up both his hands. "Try to understand, boy. I've got to fill two entire columns of the newspaper. Since this is an official day of prayer, the courts are closed. I'm going to have a harder time than usual rounding up enough stories."

It all sounded like a lot of excuses to me. I stared up at him in disgust. "Why does a fellow with as little a taste for his job—as you seem to have—want to keep it?"

"I can't afford to quit." He made a face as if he had just swallowed a spoonful of sulfur and molasses. "Let's just say that I've made some bad investments in the last few years and I owe money to a lot of people. I can only hold them off because I promise to give them a little something on my next payday. If I quit now, I'd have a pack of creditors howling after me." He gave a shudder. "It's not a pretty sight." He tipped his hat to me. "Now if you'll excuse me, I have to start making my rounds."

He began to walk down Kearney Street, then glanced over his shoulder when he heard me follow him. "And just where do you think you're going?" he asked in an annoyed voice.

"I'm sticking closer to you than your shadow until payday." I stuffed my hands into my pockets. "A police detective might not be able to squeeze money from you, but I will."

"Go away." Twain took a half-hearted swat at me, but it was easy to duck.

"It's a public sidewalk." I cautiously kept two paces behind him. "And besides, you promised I could stick with you till then."

I did not have much use for a person like him, but I did have some need of the two dollars he had promised. The only problem was collecting it, since the man was even worse than I had originally thought. I figured that I was going to have to make a real pest of myself if I was going to see that money.

"I did promise you, didn't I?" Twain smiled grimly. "Well, young Baywater, it won't be all that easy to stay with me. It's a quiet day, which means I'll have to walk and work twice as hard." He pointed toward the Plaza for proof.

The Plaza was a pleasant rectangle of grass, trees, and shrubs with diagonal paths crisscrossing it so that it looked a little like the Confederate flag. There were usually a dozen people there taking in the sun and a dozen or more hacks lined up around the Plaza waiting for fares. But today there wasn't one person to be seen in the Plaza or one hack on the street.

Even so, I wasn't impressed because I thought he was

just trying to make up more excuses. Bulldog Brill had called Mark the laziest reporter in San Francisco, and I figured that Twain just sat around most of the time.

"I can outwalk anyone," I bragged.

"Let's see." He tossed his head at me challengingly.

· CHAPTER ·

3

When we reached Commercial Street, we turned eastward. Usually the street was filled with carriages and the large, heavy wagons called drays, but today there was not one horse or wheeled vehicle between us and the ships at the Long Wharf a half mile away. The only place on the street that showed any signs of life was the *Call* Building where Twain worked. I had expected the machines in the U.S. Branch Mint to be silent; but all the merchants, warehouses, and shipping companies were also locked up tight.

Twain stood for a moment with his hands on his hips and shook his head. "This is really bad," he grumbled to me. "Looks like folks are more serious about this public praying then I first thought." He took out a cigar stub that he must have been saving. "If praying for peace becomes a habit, there's going to be many a reporter and editor out of a job." He struck a match against a streetlamp and carefully lit his cigar. Taking a long, deep pull at his cigar, he puffed out a large cloud of bluish-gray smoke. "Though, when you come right down to it, if people keep praying for peace, all the judges, police-men, and lawyers would be out of work, too—and they'd never allow *that* to happen." That thought seemed to comfort him as he took another puff at his cigar.

"There's always something happening down at the waterfront." I pointed helpfully toward the Long Wharf. "Why don't we check down there?"

He took the cigar stub from his mouth. "Good idea." He started off down the street and then paused for a moment to let me catch up. "Since we're going to be partners for a while, why don't you call me Mark."

"And I"—I drew myself up proudly—"am the Duke of Baywater, but you may address me as Your Grace."

"Your Grace, then." Mark raised his hat to me.

The waterfront was a loud, lively place because of all the ships. Unless you wanted to make the long, tiring stagecoach trip across the country, the easiest way to reach San Francisco was by ship; and any large freight had to come by sea. All the stores and warehouses along the waterfront did a brisk business. There were also a lot of saloons there, dedicated to separating the sailors from their money as quickly as possible.

For all the money that got taken in along the waterfront, you would have thought the owners would paint and spruce their places up a bit. Instead, most of the buildings were ramshackle boxes with boards rotting from the salty sea mists. Where the paint on the signboards had not flaked away already, it had begun to fade so that the words were impossible to read.

On any given day and at any given time, the waterfront's a lively place—except for that morning. The stores were all locked up tight and there wasn't any wagon traffic at all. I pulled Mark over toward a saloon called the Blue Dog Groggery. "Something's usually going on here," I said. In a funny way, I felt embarrassed that the waterfront was not living up to its reputation.

Our feet echoed emptily on the wooden planks of the sidewalk. There was hardly a soul to be seen on the street or on the piers. Even the ships riding at anchor seemed empty. I paused before the swinging doors to the Blue Dog so that I could brush off my vest and tilt my hat at a rakish angle before I shoved my way inside.

A bored-looking man with slicked-down hair was wiping large glass mugs on his dirty apron. "Sorry, Your Grace. No jobs today."

"Quite all right, my dear fellow." I mimicked an Englishman I had heard once. "Has anything noteworthy happened?"

"Nothing, Your Grace." The bartender swatted idly at a fly.

Once we were outside on the sidewalk again, Mark shoved his hat back to study me with a sad, puzzled smile. "And just who discovered your title, Your Grace? Was it your mother?"

"She never said anything about it." I began to stroll leisurely along the wooden sidewalk. "But after having given it considerable thought, I believe she must have been in hiding—maybe she was afraid of my real father's relatives. Maybe they had killed him for the title and the estates so she had to run away with me." I adjusted the brim of my hat. "It must have been something like that."

"Aren't you afraid of letting everyone know your real identity then?" Mark asked.

I stopped in front of the next saloon. "I think whatever frightened her happened a long time ago."

"And in the meantime you take jobs in saloons," Mark observed.

I shrugged. "Someone has to take up the old sawdust and put down the new."

Mark put out his cigar with two wet fingertips. "You can get awfully dirty that way, can't you?"

"It's not like I'm going to have to do it for the rest of my life." I jammed my hands into my pockets. "I'll see to that."

There was an affectionate twinkle in his eye as he put his cigar stub away. "I'll just bet you will."

There was nothing for either of us at that saloon or at the next three. The Singing Turk was a dead place, too, but the bartender there told us to help ourselves to the free lunch. It was just going to waste anyhow since there was no one there. Most of the time you had to spend a half dime† on a beer before you could touch the lunch—or I could do odd jobs in exchange for a meal.

I was all for sitting down and resting my feet, which were beginning to feel sore, but Mark said he had to keep hunting for stories. "Or," he added, "you can always catch up with me later. There's the inquest on Johnny Dougherty tonight."

I put some hard-boiled eggs into my pocket and grabbed a huge turkey drumstick. "I said I'd keep up with you and I will."

As we walked along outside, I munched at the drumstick and frowned. "They always roast their meat too long."

Mark nibbled at his. "You sound like you know the waterfront pretty well."

"I live right there." I pointed to one of the wharves.

†Silver half dimes were coins worth five cents. Nickels had not yet been coined in 1864.

Mark looked around. "Where? I don't see any buildings."

I led him to the foot of the wharf, over to one side, and pointed underneath. The pilings of the wharf had some cross beams, and over the beams I had placed some old boards I'd found. Mark got down on his knees and took off his hat so he could lean far out.

"It's a pretty nice setup," I said. "I used to have a blanket, but someone stole it."

Mark sniffed the air. "Smells a bit ripe here, doesn't it?"

"Sometimes they dump the garbage into the bay. Or fish guts and stuff," I added. "You get used to it." I waved a hand in front of us and behind us to take in the whole waterfront. "I know every rotting plank and every barnacle-covered piling on the wharves here."

"Doesn't it get cold in the wintertime?" Mark rose, dusting off his knees.

"There's always some big packing crate with straw. I can curl up in that." I took out one of the hard-boiled eggs and cracked it against the top of a piling and began to shell the egg. "And I can always go through the trash piles and get some old clothes to add to the ones I'm wearing."

Mark fingered the old patched coat I was wearing. It was about four sizes too big, and since the sleeves had had big holes in the elbows, I'd just cut the sleeves off. The gray pants I was wearing were only two sizes too big for me, and I rolled them up at the ankles; but they were so wide and floppy that they made my legs look like the legs of an elephant.

I pulled my coat out of his reach. "I go through the

trash piles anyway to sell the old clothes and rags. That's where I found this." I spread my coat open so he could see the large vest I wore. It hung on me like a tent. You could still trace the lion and unicorn pattern on the red silk, although most of the gold thread had worn away. The brass buttons had all been cut away, too, so I did my best to hold it together with safety pins. "It'll look even better once I get it fixed up."

I thought Mark had been studying my vest, but instead he pointed at the backs of my hands. "And where did you get those scars?"

I hid my hands quickly. "I catch rats and sell them to the gamblers so they can hold fights between the rats and their dogs." I shoved the hard-boiled egg into my mouth and began working my jaws up and down.

Mark made a face. "It sounds like a terrible way to make a living."

"I'm my own boss, Mark." I eyed him. "I go where I want when I want. Can you say the same?"

Mark thought about that for a while. "No, I can't," he finally had to confess with a sigh. "In fact, I might even have to join you."

We walked the hundred yards to the head of my wharf. It was cold this close to the water, and Mark buttoned up his coat. There were a dozen seagulls wheeling slowly overhead through the clean, sunlit air. The water sucked rhythmically at the pilings with soft splashing sounds, and the sun glittered on the water in little splinters of light.

Mark took off his hat and closed his eyes, turning his face to the wind so it could slip soothingly over his skin and hair. Then he opened his eyes and blinked several times. With his hat against his hip, he turned in a half circle to take in the restless waters of the bay and beyond them the brown, rolling hills of Oakland. "Y-a-a-s, well," he drawled, "there's something to be said for a home with a view." He looked down at me with grudging respect. "You're doing right well, young Baywater."

As we walked back along the wharf, I started shelling another egg. "Actually, I didn't find this place. A boy called Harry Little did. He taught me the ropes of living down here."

"And where's Harry now?" Mark had just finished eating his drumstick, so he raised the bone over his shoulder and pitched it into the water.

"He wanted to make money real quick, so he started to break into boardinghouses to steal what he could." I bit one end of the egg. "But the regular thieves caught him. They don't like competition, you see. So they took steps." I drew a finger from my left ear along my throat to my right ear.

Mark halted. "How old was he?"

"Well, I never did know for sure, but I figure he was probably about fourteen when he died."

"That's terrible." Mark looked upset.

I glanced behind me at the trail of bits of white eggshell. That was all that was left to show I'd been there. "He knew the risks."

Mark stared at me while he wiped his greasy hands on a handkerchief. "But he was your friend," Mark insisted. "Don't you care?"

"People just come and they go," I said hotly. "And no one's to stop them." I shoved the rest of the egg into my mouth.

"Your Grace," Mark said quietly, "you can't stop caring about people."

He looked real sorrowful then, like one of those foolish saints on my mother's holy cards. She had always prayed to them—a lot of good it had done her. I brushed my palms together as I finished swallowing. "And why not?" I demanded. "People just hurt one another."

Mark stretched out a hand to take my shoulder, but I dodged away from him. I was pretty good at that. His hand groped at the empty air for a moment and then it dropped to his side. "Don't judge us all by Johnny Dougherty. There's some good in the human race, after all."

"Well, I haven't seen too much of it." I hooked a thumb in my pants waistband. "And anyway," I taunted Mark, "where would you reporters be if most people weren't scum? No more robbers and murderers and no more people wanting to read about them."

I must have touched some sore spot in Mark, because instead of getting angry he only looked more upset. "That's one thing I don't like about this newspaper business. A story's only interesting if it's got one of three things in it: tears or sex or blood." He folded his handkerchief with slow, precise motions of his fingers.

"Well, it's not like I'm going to live down here forever." I took another egg from my pocket.

"You do take yourself seriously, don't you?" Mark looked at me pityingly. "Well, let me tell you something, young Baywater: A true gentleman wouldn't stop caring about folks."

I was going to ask him what a lazy spendthrift like him would know about the fine art of being a gentleman; but

I couldn't see any point in dragging out the conversation. "Let's get one thing straight." I began to shell the egg. "We just talk business from now on, all right?"

"If that's the way you want it." Mark stuffed his handkerchief into his pocket.

"I do," I said firmly.

The only problem was that there was not all that much business for us to talk about. The only exciting thing that happened during our walk was a little fire which started in a pile of trash—and even then some fool waiter put it out before it could burn more than one small box.

I was presented with a certain problem, then. I had promised Mark some action, and it seemed that I was honor-bound to produce it. "Do you want me to start another fire?"

"What?" Mark rubbed the tip of his nose with his index finger. "Since when did dukes like yourself start fires?"

"I know, but I promised you a story down here," I said. "I'm serious when it comes to keeping my word."

"Well, I guess you are." Mark did his best to fight back his smile. "But I won't hold you to it. After all, it's my job to find news, not make it."

On our way back into the city, we did find a story about a runaway horse. "This ought to be good for a dozen lines," I said. The carriage was pretty well wrapped around a lamppost, while the horse was sitting on its haunches still in its harness.

Mark, however, did not seem very cheerful. "It happens too often. At least once a day." He jotted a few notes down in his notebook and stowed it away. "Another writer once said that it was an even bet whether the trouble was caused by the horse pulling the wagon or the jackass sitting on it."

Since there was precious little going on in the heart of the city even now, Mark headed into the section of town called Little China. The Chinese had taken over the older buildings, so sometimes you would see a three-story building that would have looked right at home in New York or Boston but with Chinese ornamental balconies added to it. We stopped by the office of Ah Wae, who was the interpreter for the Chinese from Sunning District, but he did not have anything for Mark either.

By that time my feet were really hurting. "Well," I said, dragging my feet along, "do we head back for the newspaper now?" I leaned against a wall to ease the ache in my feet.

Mark stuffed his hands into his pockets. "Young Baywater," he announced with a certain smug pride, "my day has just started."

I shoved myself away from the wall. "Then I guess my day's just started, too."

He tugged at his hat brim, annoyed that he had not discouraged me after all. "I've worn out a half-dozen shadows while I've been a reporter."

"Better save your breath for walking," I told him. "Which way do we head now?" But I have to admit I was developing more respect for the man.

It was not until nearly sunset when Mark would take a rest and actually think about food. He seemed to like the fact that I had kept up with him. "You know, Your Grace," he smiled with one corner of his mouth, "you kind of grow on a person just like a barnacle on a whale."

"Thanks," I said, and added, "I guess." I could not

decide if I had been insulted or not.

I thought that we would go to some cheap little restaurant, but Mark headed right for the Occidental Hotel. I stared up at the ornate four-story walls of stucco. A row of pillars stood before the doors with handles of gleaming silver.

I looked at the hotel in awe. "You're going in there?"

"Baywater, my boy"—Mark yanked upon one of the doors—"I used to live here. But when my money ran short, I moved to a rooming house. I still board here, though. Since I didn't take time out for lunch today, I guess they owe me an extra meal."

Looking at the big hotel suddenly made me lose my nerve. "I ought to wash first," I protested. I had heard a lot of stories about the good life of a gentleman; but what I actually knew about it could have been put on the nail of my little finger.

"For all you know," Mark offered generously, "you might be the heir to one of the great estates of England."

I studied him to see if he was making fun of me, but he seemed to be dead serious. "Well," I allowed, "that remains to be proved."

"Just as," Mark winked at me, "I'm the best writer in the West—though that remains to be proved." He motioned me to enter. "I'll personally see that you get served."

Well, I realized right then that Mark Twain knew something about being a gentleman after all.

There was a cigar stand to our left as we entered, and to our right was a store that sold men's clothing. The entire lobby was covered with a plush red carpet that hushed our steps, and the mahogany paneling gleamed a rich red-brown under the huge crystal chandelier.

Some of the hotel guests turned and stared at me, whispering to one another. I think Mark knew just how nervous I was, because he leaned forward and said, "You think that they'd never seen two gentlemen like us before." There was a kindly gleam in his eye when he said that. "This way to the pride and joy of the hotel."

When Mark had led me into the dining room, he gave me a nudge. "Now this," he whispered, "is something like it, isn't it?" The walls were white stucco with red trimmings and the late twilight slipped into the room through the huge windows which were some six feet wide by fifteen feet tall. The large mahogany shutters had been folded back to allow a view of the street, where the gas streetlamps were being lit. Everything in the dining room from the windows to the decorations had been done on a grand scale, including ornamental flowers some six and a half feet wide on the ceiling far overhead.

"This way to my favorite table." Mark led me to a table by the window, and though the waiter frowned at me, he seemed to think Mark was up to one of his old tricks.

You could tell that Mark's real love in the hotel was its food. Unfortunately, we had to hurry through dinner, rushing through the chef's special consommé—a fancy name for a broth—and the main course, a bird which Mark said was grouse. It had been cooked with "apricote compote au riz Richilieu." Mark did insist that we take our time and finish our champagne sherbets, though.

When we left the hotel, the gaslit streets were filled with crowds of men and women in evening dress. Hack wheels rattled over the plank roads; and the iron shoes of the horses thundered, almost drowning out the sound of the bells of the streetcars they pulled. The cool, crisp August night was filled with a thousand voices speaking a bewildering variety of languages and dialects. You did not have to leave San Francisco to see all the peoples of the world because in San Francisco they would come to you.

Mark turned up the collar of his thin summer coat. "You know," he observed to me, "the coldest winter that I've ever spent is this summer in San Francisco."

I patted my full stomach. "Well, it ought to be warm at your office. Isn't it time to go back and write up your stories?"

Mark pulled his coat collar tighter about his throat. "I still have to cover the theaters."

I couldn't help groaning then. "Why don't you take that Bulldog Brill on your beat? That ought to convince him that you're not lazy."

Mark gave a laugh and started off down the street. "Young Baywater, compared to his schedule, I *am* lazy."

Most of what I knew about the theater could have been put into my top hat, and most of that had been learned by hanging around the melodeons and dance halls in the area.

Mark grumbled to me that first-class performers did not want to take the long hazardous, exhausting stagecoach trip across the plains and through the mountains to San Francisco; and a sea voyage was almost as dangerous. Not only was there the risk of storms, but crossing the Isthmus of Panama was a chancy business because of the diseases there. "The actors and singers who do arrive here are usually the dregs of their profession; but then," Mark added with a rueful smile, "they're not unlike some reporters who settle here."

We visited two theaters, only staying long enough each time to soak in the flavor of the performance and to take the chill from our bones before moving on. We were heading for a third when Mark suddenly came to a halt before a small restaurant that specialized in ten-cent specials. "This is Bulldog's favorite spot." He pressed his face so close to the window that his breath began to fog the glass. "Yes, there he is."

Bulldog was sitting at a table with a large white napkin tucked protectively into his collar. "I'm eating, Mark." He crammed the last bit of potato into his mouth.

"I just want to know what's happening on the Gogarty case." Mark started to reach for a biscuit, but Bulldog waved his knife and fork menacingly.

"There's still no sign of him." Bulldog began to saw away at a thick pork chop. "And that's bad for me because the boy wonder's decided to take a special interest in the case."

"Who's the boy wonder?" I asked Mark.

"Peever," Mark said, as if the name left a bad taste in his mouth. "He's the youngest district attorney anywhere in the state and he's out to make a reputation for himself as a law-and-order man. Sometimes, though, he's been in such a hurry that he hasn't always prepared his cases. In fact, some pretty dangerous criminals have gotten off because of his mistakes." Mark made another snatch at a biscuit but was waved off again by the greedy Bulldog. "To make up for that, Peever's turned his ponderous legal cannons against a few little gnats—shoplifters and vagrants—and seen that they've gotten the full penalty of the law." Mark smiled with one corner of his mouth. "I've already lit into him a few times."

"Well, he's found a new victim." Bulldog gulped some beer from a huge mug. "I think he's going to ask for murder in the first degree when we finally catch Gogarty."

Mark stiffened in outrage. "But Gogarty would've had to plan everything for it to be a first-degree murder."

Bulldog crammed more pork chop into his mouth. "So far we've only got Gogarty's word that Johnny had the bayonet. For all we know, Gogarty was the one who took the bayonet and lured Johnny up there."

Mark caught Bulldog's arm. "But the man's so simple he can barely figure out how to put on his pants."

Bulldog freed himself from Mark's grip. "Billy Gogarty is a common thug. Whether he lives or dies will be a small loss."

"Well, I aim to see that he's one man the hangman misses." Mark set his jaw stubbornly.

"And make a new reputation for yourself at the same time." Bulldog smoothed his sleeve. "I've seen too many reporters turn murder trials into such circuses that the poor defendants got lost in the crowd." Wearily he looked down at his plate. "I thought you were above that game, Mark. I'm sorry to see that I was wrong." He began to cut off another piece of his pork chop.

When Mark finally returned to the *Call* Building, he was still so angry at Bulldog and Peever that he almost ran up the three flights of stairs to the editorial office.

It was a large room dominated by a slanted desk top

that ran all the way across one wall just below the windows. A man with a neatly trimmed beard sat at one end as he scribbled away. In the center was a round, bald man with a surprised, annoyed look on his face, like a man who had just swallowed a fly by mistake. It was, Mark said later, his usual expression.

Upstairs the printers were running the press so that the clinking sounds vibrated down the walls and through the floor. Even so, the bald man managed to detect Mark sneaking over toward his desk.

Without looking up from the sheaf of papers in his hand, the bald man announced in a loud voice, "You're late, Mark. It's after eleven."

Mark did his best to stroll the rest of the way toward his part of the desk. He had to shout to make himself heard over the noise from the upstairs press. "Barnes, I do believe you could hear a gnat setting down a block away." He dropped his hat on a ledge above the desk, sending up a small flurry of notes and memos.

"If he was late," the bald man replied confidently, "I would." Suddenly the press upstairs stopped, so that the man called Barnes could speak in a more normal tone. "So what do you have for me?"

Mark took out his notebook. Standing before Barnes, he began to run through his stories, including a blast at the boy wonder. When Mark was finished, Barnes massaged his pink scalp. "Just write up what you saw, Mark. I don't want you criticizing Peever again."

Mark gripped his notebook with all the desperation of a dying man clutching his Bible. "But Peever is going to cover up the facts."

A disgusted Barnes clasped his hands in his lap.

"Whipping a DA is like beating a horse: You can only do it so many times before people start taking his side."

"All right," Mark agreed reluctantly. "But at least let me suggest the possibility that the murder might have been self-defense." Mark pointed his notebook toward me. "The boy says that both Gogarty and Dougherty may have been involved in smuggling guns."

Barnes twisted his head around and looked me up and down. "Not just on his word. He's only a little wharf rat."

"Careful what you say." Mark clamped his hand over my mouth before I could protest. "He's the Duke of Baywater," Mark said quickly. "Johnny Dougherty was his . . . uh . . . stepfather."

"Mark, I wanted you to get wrapped up in your stories"—he ran a hand over his face—"but not that wrapped up."

"I can't shake him." Mark affectionately dropped his hand away from my mouth. "I owe him money."

"Him and half the city." Barnes shook his head.

"I like owing money." Mark tried to smile. "It gives me a feeling of being wanted."

"Mark, I've always admired your talent as a writer, but you obviously don't like this job." He leaned back in his chair. "You'd be much happier investing in silver mines and such." He clapped his hands suddenly on the edge of the desk. "You're always late, and when you do get here you never have enough stories. And then you take so long to write your few stories that we have to help you."

Every now and then a muscle twitched in Mark's cheek as if he was trying to hold back some angry answer. He must have succeeded because all he did was complain, "And when I do bring you stories you tell me I can't do them." The frustration was plain in his voice.

"But you also need hard facts to back up your stories." Barnes lowered his head like a bull getting ready to charge and looked up at Mark. "Frankly, Mark, I may have to let you go if you don't start doing better. Facts, Mark." Barnes pounded a fist into his large soft palm. "We need facts and plenty of them."

Mark's shoulders rose as he took a deep breath—as if he was fighting to control his temper. Then he let his breath escape in a soft hiss. "I apologize, Your Grace," he said to me. "You were right: If I don't respect myself, how can I expect others to respect me?" He took several more breaths before he could trust himself to talk to Barnes. "If you want facts," Mark grimly promised his editor, "I'll get you facts—if I have to go through every pesthole in the city."

· CHAPTER ·

4

I waited for Mark outside the office. Since there was only one door to his place, I figured it was all right if I let him out of my sight.

I had to sit for a long time on the landing. Every now and then I could hear his editor, Barnes, shouting at him to hurry up and finish whatever story he was working on. I must have been out there at least an hour before I fell asleep.

Mark woke me by prodding me with his shoe. "Ready to go hunt up Digger?"

I stretched and yawned. I could see the office clock through the open doorway. "But it's past two in the morning. Are you really going to look for him?"

"We'll sniff around just like you originally wanted." Mark carefully lit his cigar stub. "Or does that yawn mean you're too tired?"

I got up slowly. "Just exercising my mouth muscles." To my embarrassment, I found myself yawning again.

"I wouldn't have thought they needed the extra exercise." Mark was already starting to skip down the steps so I had to hurry to catch up.

When Mark unlocked the street-level door, we found a thick fog billowing through the streets. I could not see objects more than a hundred yards away, and even the tops of buildings all around us seemed to dissolve into the silvery darkness. Streetlamps shone here and there like pale ghosts. Mark pulled up the collar on his coat. "There's just one piece of equipment we need." I followed him to a pawnshop a few buildings down.

"Hey, it's still open," I said.

"Sometimes they do their best business this late at night." Mark put his hand on the doorknob. "The gamblers need to fatten their wallets again for another try at the roulette wheel."

Guitars, dresses, and clusters of shoes were hanging together from the ceiling of the pawnshop like bunches of grapes. More items filled the shelves on either side and at the rear of the shop, leaving only a narrow hole through which the pawnbroker could handle his business.

"Evening, Tucker," Mark called.

Tucker was a tall, gangly man in his fifties who seemed to be all Adam's apple. "Payday so soon, Mr. Twain?" Tucker began to open a drawer underneath the counter.

"Didn't come to get my watch, Tucker." Mark held up his hand.

"A man rushing around like you ought to know the time." Tucker let Mark's watch dangle from his fingers like a ripe fruit.

Mark turned to a large, ceiling-high cabinet in back of one of the side counters. Behind the glass pane covering one of the shelves, he saw a clutter of guns. "I was wondering how much a small pistol might cost."

Tucker folded his arms. "Has a grammarian found you?"

"After a fashion." Mark strolled over to the counter, leaning forward so he could peer into the cabinet. "I don't need a cannon, just something to put an adequate-size hole in a man."

Tucker moved over to the cabinet and opened a glass door. "I've got just the thing for you: a five-shot Colt pocket pistol. Otherwise known as a Baby Dragoon. The entire gun is only eight inches long and weighs a little less than a pound and a half. It's all cleaned and ready to use." He took out a small pistol. "It's not too accurate at long range, but if there was that much distance between you and him, I suppose you'd be taking to your heels first."

"You could bet the shop on it, Tucker." Mark took the gun from him and pretended to aim it at a clock. "The balance feels a little clumsy." He checked the tag attached by a string to the trigger guard. "But the price is right." He set the gun down on the counter. "You wouldn't consider an IOU, would you?"

Tucker was suddenly less friendly. "Strictly cash, Mr. Twain."

"It's a fine how-de-do," Mark complained, "when you'll trust complete strangers before you'll trust your friends." He rubbed his chin for a moment as if taking Tucker's measure. "*The* Pritchard is coming back to town for a revival of her play."

I'd heard about an actress by the name of Barrie Pritchard. The whole city had, in fact. Last year she had done a play dressed only in flesh-colored tights.

Tucker shrugged. "I've already reserved my tickets."

"Like to meet her?" Mark asked shrewdly. "My editor doesn't think she's refined enough for his critical sensibilities so I'll probably have to review the play. As a drama critic, I could get backstage." He nudged Tucker. "I'll take you along." He paused, pleased to see how Tucker's mouth had opened, and then added, "For an interview."

Tucker's mouth had opened even wider. "You could do that?"

"Of course." Behind the counter, Mark had crossed his fingers.

Tucker took out a small rectangular box of cartridges and a flat cylindrical box of percussion caps. "I suppose you'll need some of these, too."

"They might help," Mark agreed, and began to load the gun.

When Mark was finished, Tucker wagged a finger at him. "Now remember, Mr. Twain, you've got to get me backstage."

"You'll get as far as I do." Mark winked at him. Outside the pawnshop, Mark took a long, deep breath.

"I thought you told nothing but the truth," I said to him.

"Or a reasonable facsimile of it." Mark stowed the gun away in his coat pocket and gave it a smug pat. "Now let's go find this Digger."

We didn't have much luck at the first two places we tried, so I led Mark to a quiet street full of rickety-looking buildings of wood or rusted corrugated iron, all of which seemed waiting for the next earthquake to put them out of their misery. Most of the buildings stood empty now, and over the years the planks of the street had either been splintered by heavy wagons or slowly buried by mud until the street seemed like a dirt road again. The only decoration was a tilted hitching post in the middle of the block.

The Rogers Drayage Company was a small, one-story building with a narrow wooden front. To the right, between the drayer's and a warehouse, was a narrow alley, hardly more than a foot wide, into which the entire neighborhood seemed to have dumped its trash so that the garbage and debris lay ankle-deep. Bright light spilled from the windows of the company.

"I wish there was a way we could have brought Bulldog along." Licking his fingers, Mark pinched out his cigar and put it away.

Suddenly a desperate voice began to shout. "Honest, Digger, I didn't tell them nothing."

"That's Billy," I said.

Mark put one hand into his coat pocket. "I'm not getting the police until I'm sure."

As we crept toward the building, we could just make out someone answering Billy. "There's only one way to quit this scheme," a man with an Australian accent was saying, "and that's a quick trip to the cemetery." By that time, we were right beneath the window.

"I came here because I trusted you," Billy complained.

"Yeah, well, we all make mistakes, Gogarty."

Mark was motioning for us both to leave when the roar of a pistol made me almost jump right out of my shoes. As it was, I couldn't help straightening up to peek through one of the dusty window panes.

Billy was lying on his back, his mouth and eyes still open as if in silent, angry protest at the bloody hole in his chest.

Standing over him was Digger, a tall blond man with a face the color of raw beef. Though he wore a collarless shirt with a dirty vest of green serge, he had on a very expensive pair of knee-high boots—probably stolen from a rich man's corpse. In his hand was a navy Colt revolver.

"That lowdown skunk," I muttered, and would have

said more except that Mark put a hand on my shoulder. "Steady now," he whispered. "We've got our own skins to worry about."

"This Gogarty business is going to cost you a hundred extra," Digger announced.

Glaring at Digger were two strangers. The first was a lean whipcord of a man with a face that had the look of old, worn leather.

"We already paid you your money," he growled.

Digger leaned back against the wheel of one of the two huge drays behind him. "That was for getting off the shipment. A job like this costs extra." He held up a hand. "And don't give me one of your speeches about the Cause. I'm not one of your Johnny Rebs: I'm a businessman."

Mark excitedly poked me in the ribs. "Digger must be smuggling something for the Confederates."

The second stranger was a man in his mid-twenties with a gentlemanly air to him. He stood with his right heel against the instep of his left foot; and he was dressed in a well-tailored, double-breasted coat that reached to his thighs and twill pants that were tucked into an elegant pair of Wellington boots with their front flaps turned down. His mustache was precisely trimmed and waxed to sharp points.

"My dear fellow"—the young man spoke in a calm, almost indifferent voice—"Gogarty was your man. Hence he was your responsibility."

"How was I supposed to know that Gogarty'd kill Johnny instead of the other way around." An embarrassed Digger tugged at his ear. "I still had to pay Johnny before he'd try it. That means I've lost money out of my own pocket, Major."

"I think you overestimate your worth to us, sir." The young major casually raised his hand and the leather-faced man snatched a Le Mat pistol from behind his back. Le Mats were big guns with two barrels. They fired nine shots from the upper barrel and a .60–shot charge from the lower barrel.

I'll give this to Digger: He did not seem afraid. He simply raised one foot, letting it swing back and forth on the heel. "I'm disappointed in you, Major. I thought you was a gent." Turning his head to one side, he called behind him. "Come out and say hello, Felix." Wearing civilian clothes, Felix rose from inside the nearest dray. In his hand was a shotgun, both barrels aimed at the young major. I should have known that Felix was tied into this mess somehow.

For a long time, the place was as quiet as a church. The major seemed almost embarrassed, as if Digger had said something rather rude. Finally the major scratched the tip of his nose and then slowly lowered his hand. Reluctantly the leather-faced man stowed his pistol away. "I'll see that you get your money in an hour." His voice was suddenly all golden butter and sweet honey. "Would that be satisfactory, sir?"

"That's fine." Digger planted his feet firmly. "But remember, if you don't pay me by one tomorrow, I'll do some singing for the coppers."

"Most certainly." The major nodded to Digger and began walking toward the door. Crouching down, Mark and I ran to the narrow alley between the drayer's and the warehouse next door. I went first, flattening myself against the wall as I edged into the alley. I went on until both Mark and I were hidden completely in the darkness. A moment later, I heard a door creak open and heard the hurried footsteps of the two Confederates as they passed by.

"What . . ." I began, but Mark pressed his fingers over my mouth. He had a hunch about something, and I'm glad that he did, because a minute later I heard the door creak open again and another man slipped up the street, apparently trailing the Confederates.

"That was Felix," Mark explained to me. "I suppose he's going to make sure they get the money."

Mark began to slide back along the alley. "Let's go get the police and lay an ambush for the whole gang."

But I tugged at his coat. "Whoa there. It'd just be our word against Digger's. He could even claim to be a hero for killing Billy."

Mark took off his hat and leaned his head back against the wall. "You're right." He braced his feet against the junk in the alley. "Don't tell me we have to wait all night to catch them with something."

"You've got a pistol." I pointed at his bulging coat pocket. "Let's get a confession from Digger."

"Bulldog said he was awfully dangerous," Mark objected.

"Then you give me the pistol and I'll get the confession." I started to reach for his hip but he jammed his hand into his pocket.

"No, we're in this together." Mark held onto his pistol as if it were a magical charm that would protect him. Slowly Mark edged his way back to the mouth of the alley. He poked his head outside cautiously. "All clear," he whispered to me.

We crept out onto the street and back toward the window. At first, I couldn't see Digger at all, only the shotgun leaning against a wheel of one of the drays.

Then I saw a door open in the back and Digger appeared with some papers in his hand. With his boot he cleared a space on the dirt floor and then took a kerosene lamp from its nail on a nearby post.

"Maybe that's evidence. Get your gun out." I headed for the man-size door that had been built within the large double set of stable doors.

"Wait up," Mark called.

But I'd had enough of his caution. Those papers might be just the thing we needed. Trying the knob, I found it wasn't locked. I checked behind me. Mark already had his pistol in his hand so I jerked the door open and stepped into the room. Mark stumbled in after me.

Digger was kneeling in the dirt. He'd raised the glass chimney of the kerosene lamp so that the flame was exposed.

"Put those papers down." Mark raised his pistol.

Digger thrust the handful of papers toward the flames so that they caught on fire. Then he let them drop to the dirt. I ran forward to stomp out the fire. "You're in my way," Mark shouted to me. I dropped to the ground immediately.

"I wouldn't worry, lad." Digger jerked his navy Colt from the waistband of his pants. Digger's gun looked huge compared to Mark's little pocket pistol. "That gent has to cock the hammer before that little peashooter of his will fire." Digger thumbed back the hammer of his own gun with a loud click.

I was scuttling on all fours toward the drays as I heard Mark pull back the hammer of his own gun. "I forgot," Mark said. When I reached the drays, I got hold of the shotgun. It was so big and heavy that it was hard to keep the gun from dragging in the dirt as I slid underneath the dray. I was afraid that dirt might have clogged the barrels so that the shotgun might explode in my face when I tried to fire it.

Mark was standing there with his gun aimed at Digger, but he just didn't seem able to make his finger move the necessary fraction of an inch to pull the trigger. Digger was really enjoying himself—like a cat playing with a mouse. He aimed his own pistol leisurely at Mark.

I did not wait for any more. I rested the heavy barrels of the shotgun on a spoke of the dray's wheel and pulled back the twin hammers. Digger whirled around and saw me just as I pulled both triggers.

There were twin flashes of light and a loud deafening explosion. Digger was thrown toward a stall like a doll—even as I was knocked flat on my back by the recoil of the shotgun. I lay for a moment, listening to the four horses neighing excitedly in their stalls, their hooves thudding heavily against the wooden walls. Then, using the large rim of the wheel, I pulled myself up to a sitting position.

Mark lowered the hammer of his pistol and walked over to me. "Are you all right?"

I probed with my fingers at my shoulder. "The shotgun butt hit me pretty hard, but I don't think anything's broken. Just bruised."

"You saved my life, you know." Mark put the pistol away in his coat pocket and helped me slide out from under the dray.

Beyond the blackened ashes I saw Digger, lying on his back, his eyes staring at me. His pistol lay a yard away from his hand. "Is he? . . ."

"Pretty thoroughly," Mark said.

"He's the first man I ever killed." I started to shake.

"Let's hope it's your last." Mark tried to put a hand on my shoulder, but I shied away from him.

Blood was beginning to spread from the wounds in Digger's chest. Suddenly the stable felt icy cold, and I wrapped my arms around myself.

Mark scratched his throat thoughtfully. "Y-a-a-s, well," he said slowly and with care, as if he was having a hard time speaking, "you know, when the war started, I joined up right away in a local outfit. We called ourselves the Marion Rangers because we came from Marion County. It was a fancy title for a ragtag bunch. One night we thought we'd play soldier and shot at what we thought was a Yankee cavalryman." Mark swung the side of his foot slowly back and forth across the dirt floor of the stable. "When we went to the corpse later, we found that he didn't have either a uniform or a weapon."

"And what happened?" My own voice felt awkward and scratchy.

"We . . . we just stood around him and watched him die because there wasn't any way of saving him." Mark scratched at his forehead with his thumb. "I left for Nevada after that." He smiled at me weakly. "So you're not alone."

"But you're not sure your bullet killed that man," I argued. "I know my shot did."

"But my man might have been an innocent rider," Mark countered stubbornly. "On the other hand, Digger's probably done a dozen things that should have put a noose around his neck." Mark suddenly stopped and snorted. "Listen to what we're arguing about: which one of us is the guiltier one."

He took out his cigar stub. There was only about an

inch left. When he tried to light it, his hand shook. Until
then I had not realized he was just as upset as I was.
After two puffs, he flung it away from him. Even he
could not nurse that cigar stub along anymore.

It's funny, but I felt closer to Mark at that moment
than I had to anyone since my mother died. Though
Harry had been friendly and kind enough, there had
always been a rough edge to him because he always
lorded his superior waterfront knowledge over me.

"We're two sad specimens, all right." I nodded to
Mark.

This time when Mark reached out, I let him pat my
shoulder clumsily. Without having to say it, I think we
both knew we were loners: restless people who would
never feel comfortable in a crowd—nor have a crowd
feel very comfortable with us. "We'll make out somehow, you and me."

"What about the papers?" I went over to the kerosene
lamp, but by that time the papers seemed to be all ash.
I'm a scavenger both by nature and by trade, I guess. I
couldn't help poking around with my toe in the ashes.
Against all that blackness a little scrap of white stood
out real clear.

"Mark"—I picked it up—"look at this."

Mark came over excitedly. He took it between trem-
bling fingers, trying not to crumble any more of the
fragile paper. There, in plain script, it said: ". . . our raid
on the M. . . ."

He slipped the scrap protectively between two pages of
his notebook and stowed it away inside a coat pocket.
"What do you think the *M* stands for? *M* as in powder
magazine—like the one at Black Point?" After all, Billy

and Johnny had been stationed there.

"Could be anything," I shrugged. "Let's go get the police now."

But finding a policeman in that part of town was easier said than done. They rarely went there because it was a popular area for smugglers who were willing to pay hefty bribes to the dishonest policemen and to murder the honest ones. It took nearly an hour before we found a pair of policemen and brought them back to the Rogers Drayage Company.

I knew something was wrong when we found the door locked. As one of the patrolmen experimented with the ring of skeleton keys he had taken from his pocket, I stared at the darkened windows. "I was sure we left it unlocked and the lanterns lit."

The second patrolman rocked back and forth on his heels as he studied Mark. "Haven't I seen you somewhere before?"

"Probably. I'm a reporter," Mark explained nervously, "so I'm in and out of the police station a lot."

The patrolman cocked his head to the side. "And what would your name be, sir?"

"Mark Twain." Mark quickly added, "But this isn't any hoax. Two men have been killed. One of them was Billy Gogarty. Ask the boy here."

The patrolman turned to me. "And what would your name be, lad?"

"I am His Grace, the Duke of Baywater."

The two patrolmen exchanged glances. There was an uncomfortable silence as the first patrolman finally turned a key successfully in the lock and jerked the door open. Locating a lantern near the door, he lit it. Crowding into the doorway, Mark and I could both see that the drays and the horses were gone.

The first patrolman slowly surveyed the gloomy building. "And where was this corpse?"

Mark entered the building, pointing to the spot near the stalls. "He was right there." He walked over to the spot and crouched. "See, someone's dug up the dirt and put down fresh earth in its place." He sifted through the still damp soil. "The Confederates must have come back with Digger's money. I guess they had all the time they needed to hide the evidence and cart the bodies away in the drays to hide somewhere." Mark raised his hands to gesture at the walls. "But I'll just bet they didn't have the time to get the shotgun pellets from the boards."

"There's many a building around here with bullet holes." Unimpressed, the first patrolman motioned for us to move back to the door and waited until we had exited before he blew out the light in the lantern.

Mark thrust his hand into his pocket. "Look, we've even got a scrap of paper with part of their plans on it."

"To be sure." The patrolman shut the door behind him and used his skeleton keys to relock the door. "My mother used to tell me an old saying, 'Fool me once, shame on you. Fool me twice, shame on me.' You're lucky I don't run you in for malicious mischief, but you're not worth the paperwork."

Mark angrily squared his shoulders, as if he were getting ready for a fight. "But—"

No one wins an argument with the police, so I tugged at his arm. "Let's go, Mark."

"I'm talking to these two." Mark tried to shake free, but I had a good grip on his arm.

"You'll just get into trouble if you argue," I insisted quietly.

"You listen to the young fellow," the first patrolman advised Mark. He nodded to his partner and they disappeared into the fog.

Mark took several long, deep breaths until their footsteps had faded away. "Well, you saved me again, young Baywater. This is getting to be a habit with you, isn't it?"

The gray, pearly mist was even thicker now. It curled in wisps like ghosts, ghosts that reached outward with Digger's hands. I found myself straining my ears for footsteps. "Do you think those rebs will come back for us?"

"They could," Mark admitted. "Maybe we ought to stick together. You can sleep on the floor of my room tonight."

"What makes you think it'd be any safer at your place than at mine?" I demanded.

"Because, young Baywater, old boy"—Mark bowed and flourished his hat toward the south—"they would never be able to find us in the mess in my room. Besides," he winked at me, "how do you know you'll ever be able to catch up with me tomorrow?"

"That's right. It's payday, isn't it?" I didn't much like the idea of sleeping alone that night, not with a couple of vengeful Confederates loose in the city. On the other hand, I did not want Mark to think that I needed protection. "Well," I pretended to grumble, "just for tonight then."

·CHAPTER·
5

It was a little after seven in the morning when we burst into the office of Bulldog Brill. The startled detective stared at Mark for a moment and then took out his watch to consult it. "Mark, what are you doing up before eight—or," he said, as if a new thought had struck him, "haven't you been to sleep yet?"

Mark planted both his fists upon the detective's desk. "Billy Gogarty and Digger were both killed last night."

Instead of showing even mild curiousity, Bulldog simply laughed. "I heard about that little escapade. The story was all over the station about how you tried to hoax those two patrolmen with disappearing corpses."

Mark straightened. "It's not a hoax, Bulldog. I swear."

"Look, Mark, even if it's true, neither of them will be missed." Bulldog set his feet on top of his desk as he slouched back in his chair. "In fact, I may even celebrate with a little party."

Mark took out his notebook and spread its pages to reveal the scrap of paper. "Then what about the Confederates? They're not likely to shelve their plans just because Digger is dead."

"What plans?" Bulldog put his hands behind his head.

"There's going to be a raid on something that begins with the letter *M*." Mark pointed eagerly toward the burnt scrap. "That soldier, Felix Pettibone, could tell you about the plot."

"It would just be your word against his—and do I have to tell you what yours is worth?" Bulldog simply sat there with a big smirk on his face.

Something seemed to snap inside of Mark. He shoved the detective's feet from his desk so that his heels crashed against the floor. "Why doesn't anyone believe me?"

"Maybe"—Bulldog slowly and deliberately planted his feet back on top of his desk—"I ought to put you into a cell so you can figure that out for yourself."

"No need. We're leaving." Mark carefully closed his notebook and put it away. "But you're going to feel like a jackass when I plaster the story all over the front page of the newspaper." He motioned me toward the door.

It was only a short walk from the police station over to the *Call* Building. When Mark walked into the office, Barnes glanced at the clock on the wall and then took out his watch, staring at it, perplexed, and giving it a shake. "It can't be," he muttered.

"I don't see why everyone has to make such a fuss," Mark grumbled. "I've been known to get up early."

"Only as an omen of disaster like falling stars and blood-red moons." Barnes began to write something on a sheet of paper. "But thank God you came in early. I was just about to go over to the Broadway Street wharf. I've just gotten a hot tip. The *Rapidan* caught a bunch of gun smugglers on the *Haze* last night." He thrust the note into Mark's hand. "And before you start crowing, keep in mind that there's nothing to connect Gogarty with this caper."

Mark took out the scrap of paper excitedly. "But maybe I do have something after all. Last night I made investigative history." He glanced at me. "Or rather we did. Digger was talking to these two Confederates at his place about a shipment of some kind."

Barnes looked at the scrap of paper. "You've reported this to the police?"

Mark couldn't look him in the face. "I did. They didn't believe me."

"Then you can hardly expect me to." Barnes turned back to his desk and pretended to be very interested in the work there.

"But you will." Mark determinedly put the scrap of paper away in his pocket. Glancing at the note Barnes had given him, Mark steered me toward the door. "I'll get all the evidence I need at the *Rapidan*."

There was a streetcar rumbling along when we reached Sansome Street. "Let's see if you're game enough to stick with me." Mark might have been twenty-eight, but there was still a lot of boy in him. He ran right out into the street, dodging in front of a cursing hackman, and managed to jump on board the streetcar. I followed a moment later.

The conductor frowned. "There would have been another car along in ten minutes." Then he recognized Mark. "Oh, it's you, Mr. Twain." He held out his hand for our fares. "Busy as usual?"

"Trying not to let the moss grow on me, Cal." Mark reached into his pocket. His hand stayed there as he glanced at me in embarrassment. "I don't suppose you . . . uh. . . ."

I dug two half dimes from my pocket and handed them to the conductor. "Why couldn't we walk?"

Mark found a seat and slumped down on it. "I'm a reporter on a hot story. Time and the presses wait for no one."

"No wonder you've got all those debts if you throw it around like this. You owe me two dollars and ten cents now." I sat down beside him, listening to the steady clopping of the horses' hooves as they pulled the streetcar along the tracks.

The huge pile driver at the foot of the Broadway Street Wharf was still silent, as it was too early for its work crew. The ground had collapsed there, so huge, forty-five-foot wooden poles were being driven deep into the earth before the hole was filled in. However, neither the hole nor the stack of pilings seemed to stop the bustling traffic on the waterfront. I couldn't help remembering how empty it had been yesterday.

Two wagons, hitched together to carry a new sailing mast to a ship, slowly rumbled by. Mark ducked between the wagons, ignoring the teamsters' curses. He gave a laugh when he saw that I'd managed to stay right on his heels.

He was still feeling frisky. "Keep up with me if you can," he called over his shoulder. He began to pick his way across the sidewalk display of a ship's chandler—the storekeeper who outfitted ships. There were ropes, cables, chains, blocks, anchors, and small boats called dories, and even a whaleboat. I followed Mark across them all.

Skirting along the edge of the cave-in, we made it to the long Broadway Street Wharf. To our right several Whitehall boatmen waited to take customers out to various ships at anchor in the bay. To our left, a large white ferryboat sat by the wharf like a fat pigeon sleeping in the morning sun. It would carry passengers across the bay up one of the rivers.

Mark slowed as we passed it. "She's a bit rounder," Mark said dreamily, "but she reminds me a little of the riverboats I used to pilot." He sighed softly. "It's a shame the war came along and stopped traffic on the Mississippi."

The *Rapidan* was a tug that lay about halfway up the wharf where we found a Lieutenant Bainbridge in charge. He was a fussy, straight-backed, middle-aged man who smiled gruffly at us as soon as he learned who Mark was. "Sorry to disappoint you, but we did our job, didn't we?"

"Pardon?" Mark asked politely.

The lieutenant clasped his hands behind his back impatiently. "Ever since the *Chapman* affair, you reporters have been screaming like bad sopranos about how unprotected the harbor is."

Mark tapped his pencil against his lip. "Well, I wasn't a reporter here at the time, but as I recall the Confederates outfitted a ship called the *Chapman* right in San Francisco Bay under everyone's nose. And it was only by the purest luck that a navy ship was here temporarily and caught the *Chapman* before it began raiding our shipping."

"We did our job then," the lieutenant said stiffly, "and we did it again last night." He rocked up and down on the balls of his feet. "The navy may not move as fast as you civilians may want, but we get things done." Then, with grudging pride, he told Mark how the port authorities had been on the watch for anything suspicious. With a squad of soldiers on board the *Rapidan*, he had boarded the *Haze* south of San Francisco at Half Moon Bay and confiscated four thousand guns and a ton or more of ammunition. The ship and its illegal cargo had been taken to Alcatraz, where she now lay at anchor under the shadow of the island's guns.

"Instead of scolding the navy all the time, you ought to take on the courts." The lieutenant jabbed a finger at Mark. "If the courts would do more than slap the wrists of these smugglers, we could put them away for good." The lieutenant rubbed the back of his neck. "Hell, there was a man on board the *Haze* that we'd caught once before on the *Chapman*. He should never have been out on the streets."

Mark began writing feverishly in his notebook. "You mean, the Confederates might be behind this smuggling operation?" Mark looked excitedly at the lieutenant. "Do you think they could have been trying to land the guns there? After all"—Mark began to tick his reasons off on his fingers—"they say the area south of Half Moon Bay is full of Confederate sympathizers. Some of them even fly the Confederate flag. And just last month, there was a Confederate guerrilla called Fletcher who was robbing stages around there."

The lieutenant raised his hands in alarm. "Now hold on there. The city's already frightened enough without starting up some new scare."

Mark turned the pages of his notebook until he found the scrap of paper. "But we've got evidence about some kind of raid by the Confederates." He held it out hopefully to the lieutenant. "Maybe they've got a secret army down there."

The lieutenant spread his legs slightly as if getting ready for a fight. "The army has sent every available man down to that area to check. If anything is there, they'll find it. In the meantime"—he wagged a warning finger at Mark—"if you try to quote me about the Confederates, I'll not only deny it, I'll have you up on charges of inciting a riot." He gave Mark a rude shove. "Now get off my ship."

When we were back on the wharf, Mark kicked a heel against a worn plank. "Well, I guess the major wasn't going to raid the powder magazine at Black Point. If the rebs had enough powder and ball for four thousand muskets, they didn't need any more."

"It's hard to think on an empty stomach," I said.

Mark grinned. "You're a man after my own heart, Your Grace."

At the Occidental Hotel, we split a breakfast plate— Mark took the salmon and fried oysters which weren't to my taste at all, while I had the fried eggs and bacon. I began to spread as much jam as I could pile onto a piece of toast. "Supposing the major does have an army outside the city, what other targets begin with an *M?*"

With his fork Mark carefully began to separate the thin white bones from his piece of salmon. "Well, there's General McDowell, the new head of the Department of the Pacific. I hear he's a good general, just unlucky."

"Maybe they are planning a kidnapping." I took an excited bite from my toast.

Mark speared a forkful of red salmon. "Well, it might confuse things if the general and his staff were to disappear." He slipped his fork inside his mouth and chewed thoughtfully.

I picked up a piece of crisp bacon and crunched it between my teeth. "Sure, kidnap the head general so he can't organize a defense against an attack."

"That's true," Mark sighed. "Heaven knows this city is wide open to an attack from both the land and the sea." Between forkfuls of salmon, Mark told me about a tour of the harbor defenses which General McDowell had conducted last month. The poor general had made the mistake of trusting his aides' glowing reports. Instead he had found cannon placed so poorly that a child with a slingshot could have taken them out of action. Other guns had not been taken out of storage. Even the guns of the formidable Fort Point were questionable because the fuses on their shells had made the shells explode almost the moment they left the mouths of the cannon. General McDowell had come away from the tour shaken to the very soles of his soldierly boots.

"It wasn't his fault, really," Mark explained. "The harbor was supposed to be defended by the *Camanche*."

"Well, where is she?" I asked.

"They dismantled the *Camanche* back east"—Mark wiped his mouth with his napkin—"and packed all the pieces into the hold of a ship and sent it here. The ship made it past the Confederate privateers, through the storms of the Atlantic, and around the Horn"—he motioned to a waiter and pointed to his almost empty coffee cup—"only to sink once it was safe and snug at a pier in San Francisco Bay."

I put my hands on my waist and slowly sat back. "Doesn't that sound awfully funny to you?"

"At the time, they said it was an unusually strong wind that did it." Mark nodded his thanks to the waiter who refilled his cup. "They salvaged the pieces of the *Ca-manche* two months ago."

I scratched behind my ear. "What's so special about this *Camanche?*"

Mark drained his coffee from his cup and set it down. "She's an ironclad monitor."†

"Monitor." I mouthed the word slowly.

"Monitor." Mark parroted me and then threw his napkin on the table. "The *Camanche* is being reassembled at a shipyard. The major probably wants to get in there and destroy her once and for all."

"Only Billy got cold feet." I flung my napkin down on top of Mark's. "He was scared of hanging for treason."

Mark shoved himself away from the table. "We've got to go right out to the Presidio."

"But that's all the way on the other side of the peninsula," I protested. "Why do we have to go there?"

Mark was already heading for the door. "Because the army has its headquarters there. They'll stop the major."

From a livery man that Mark knew, we borrowed a small carriage. I'd hitched rides on the backs of carriages before as a kind of game with some of the other kids. It was my first time actually sitting in one. In fact, it was the first time that I could remember when I had actually left San Francisco.

It didn't take long to leave the western edge of the city at Larkin Street. Before us lay the gently rising slope of another hill, barren except for some damp brown weeds. I could see the shreds of fog hovering near its top, getting

†A monitor was a type of armored ship which mounted two guns in a rotating turret so that it looked like a round cake on a tray.

ready to slip across the city once the sun had set.

Beyond the hill, a high, dense fog blocked the sun completely. Nothing but rolling sand dunes lay between us and the Pacific Ocean. I strained my eyes trying to catch a glimpse of the ocean waves, but I couldn't. The only moving thing was a slight breeze, blowing little sand sprites up and then down the curve of the dunes.

"Looking for someone?"

"I was just trying to see the ocean." I slumped back against the worn leather seat.

Mark held the reins lightly. "Haven't you ever been out there?"

I shrugged. "It's just salt water—like the bay."

"Oh, no, it's a lot different. Bigger. Lonelier." He grinned at me. "We'll go sometime when all this crazy business is finished."

I wiped at my nose trying to figure out Mark's angle. I'd never had a promise like that before. "Really?"

He nudged me with his elbow. "Want me to swear to it?"

"I wouldn't want you to wear out your credit in heaven," I said.

"I may be bad about paying back folks"—Mark sounded hurt—"but I keep my other promises."

When we finally got to the Presidio, the sentry recognized Mark from his other visits and waved him through the gates. Mark turned the carriage onto a path that wound its way down the barren slopes to a cluster of white, two-story buildings. Soldiers were busy drilling on the level ground there.

Mark gave a chuckle. "I'd like to see the major's face when he finds a company of those boys waiting for him."

Tying the horse to a hitching post, Mark headed straight for the largest building where he asked for a certain officer. However, an efficient-looking sergeant informed us that the man had been transferred and instead ushered us into the office of a Captain Purdy. The office was almost overfurnished with a massive mahogany desk, chairs, and shelves. Every spare square inch of wall space was taken up with lithographs of prominent Union men from Lincoln on down. Heavy, blue-velvet drapes had been drawn back from the windows to reveal the whitecaps on the bay.

Captain Purdy was a large man in an unbuttoned coat. He rose and extended his hand with all the energy and warmth of a man running for mayor. "Always happy to meet a member of the press, Mister?. . . "

"Twain." Mark closed the door behind him. "Mark Twain. Of the *Daily Morning Call.*"

The captain's hand dropped to his side, and he sat down. "So you're Mark Twain."

"You've heard of me?" Cautiously Mark took one chair. I took the other.

"Lots of times." Captain Purdy laced his fingers together and set them on top of his desk. "I've got a sister in Nevada."

"Oh?" Mark shrank a little in his chair. "Do I know her?"

"Probably. Her name's Mrs. Danley and she's pretty active in the charities." The captain began rubbing his palms together. "But in any event, she certainly knows you." The captain pressed his lips in a thin, bloodless smile. "Too bad you didn't go to that duel. I'm told your opponent was a deadly shot."

Mark rubbed his chin. "Are you from back east?"

"New York," the captain declared proudly.

"Y-a-a-s, well, I thought so." Mark folded his arms. "They don't know much about manners back there, do they?"

The captain straightened a sheaf of papers. "Why don't you state your business so you can get out of my office?"

"There are these Confederate raiders, you see." Mark waited for the captain to explode, but Purdy suddenly seemed to have grown a long fuse. Encouraged, Mark took the scrap of paper from his notebook and began to outline yesterday's events from the killing of Johnny Dougherty to the deaths of Billy and Digger. "Digger was burning some papers. This was the only thing we managed to save, but you can see for yourself what it says." Mark handed the paper scrap to the captain. "We have reason to believe that the *Haze* was just a diversion to draw your men to the south while the raiders hit their target here."

"What target?" the captain demanded. He was all business now as he reached into a humidor and took out a fat cigar.

Mark stared longingly at the humidor. "We're not sure. They might be planning to kidnap General McDowell and his staff."

"Small loss there. They're always in the way." The captain bit off one end of his cigar and spat it out. "But don't you dare quote me."

Mark and I exchanged glances. The captain had just knocked down one of our theories. "Well, if that's the case"—Mark shifted uneasily in his chair—"the Confederates probably mean to destroy the *Camanche* before it's finished being rebuilt." Mark pointed eagerly at the scrap of paper. "She's a monitor."

Purdy lit his cigar. As the smoke began to wreathe about his head, the captain studied the scrap of paper. It looked so tiny on top of his broad desk. Finally he took the cigar from his mouth and looked at Mark. "Just one thing bothers me, Twain. Why didn't the police come here with you?"

Mark suddenly looked as if he were caught in a trap— and the trap was of his own making by just one thoughtless story written in Nevada. "Those damn fools don't believe me. You see, Billy and Digger's bodies disappeared and. . . ." His words trailed off as Captain Purdy picked up the scrap of paper and set it in a large ashtray.

"Congratulations, Twain, you nearly sold me." The captain touched his cigar to the paper in the ashtray. With a puff of smoke, it caught fire. It didn't take long for it to disappear into ash. "I suppose you were going to see the police next and tell them everything that I was doing so the police would finally believe you. And with the police behind you, you'd have the whole city foxed."

Mark got up angrily from his chair. "Now wait a moment. That last hoax nearly ruined me. Why would I want to start another one?"

Ignoring Mark, the captain rose and crossed the room toward the door. "There's no use trying to see the provost marshal or General McDowell." He jerked the door open. "All their visitors are referred through me." He looked at Mark warningly. "And this being a state of war, we don't like having strangers wander around the Presidio."

"I'm glad to see you're worried about something," Mark snapped as we left the office.

Mark did not say much on the way back to the city. I thought lunch would perk him up, but we had no sooner entered the lobby of the Occidental Hotel than a little fish-eyed man called us over to the cigar stand. "Mr. Twain." He waved to Mark urgently. "Mr. Twain."

"This is all I need," Mark grumbled.

Norton I, Emperor of the United States and Protector of Mexico, was already at the cigar stand when we walked over. He had once been a rich merchant; but when he lost all his money, he had gone crazy, and he now lived on the charity of the entire city. Dressed in a long blue officer's coat with gold epaulets and a beaver hat with a feather and a rosette, he held a black umbrella and a hickory cane in one hand while he selected a cigar with the other. "Thank you," he said to the little fish-eyed man. "Everyone will know that you have the imperial custom, Ferris."

"That's very kind of you, Your Highness." Ferris gave a little indulgent bow.

If you ask me, he gave a bad name to truly titled people who also were willing to earn their own living; but I wasn't in the mood for an argument. "Your Highness," I nodded to him.

He lifted his head with imperial disdain and looked down at me. "Your Grace," he said, and strutted away.

Mark tapped his fingers impatiently on the glass top of the counter. "I know all about my bill, Ferris. I'll settle it tomorrow."

"Well, I wouldn't refuse anything you could pay me."

Ferris took out a blue envelope from his coat pocket. "But I called you over because a gentleman left this letter for you. He said it was very important."

Mark held the envelope with very little enthusiasm. "It's probably someone with a hot investment tip—only they always seem to go cold as soon as I've put my money into them." Mark moodily rubbed the envelope between his fingers. "Do you remember what he looked like?"

"I'm afraid not, Mr. Twain." Ferris glanced at the humidor which he had carelessly left on top of his glass counter within reach of Mark's hand. Too late he realized his mistake.

Mark slipped the envelope into his pocket with one hand and with the other lifted the humidor's lid. "Just put the cigars on my bill, will you, Ferris?"

Ferris slapped his hand over the mouth of the humidor. "I'm sorry, Mr. Twain, but your bill is already outstanding."

"I told you that I'd take care of it." Mark set the lid down on the counter. "I get paid tonight so I'll have the money tomorrow."

Ferris, however, kept his hand over the humidor. "I surely hope so. It's been a long time since I even saw a dime from you, Mr. Twain."

Mark frowned; but when he saw the hardening corners of Ferris's mouth, Mark apparently decided not to argue. "You know what I ought to do?" he asked bitterly. He didn't wait for a response from Ferris or me. "I ought to declare myself the heir apparent to Emperor Norton. He never has trouble getting credit."

"The emperor," Ferris declared with great dignity,

"never asks for very much."

Mark stared at the humidor. He felt sadly around in his pockets for any kind of spare change, but could find none. In desperation he turned to me. "The more something's denied to you, the more you want it. You're a man of the world. You know how that feels."

I crossed my arms over my chest. "Up until now I've usually been '*young* Baywater.'"

"I stand corrected, Your Grace." Mark bowed his head slightly and glanced at me with mock humility. "What do you say?"

"Sure." Grandly I slapped some change on top of the counter. "I'll buy one straight out for the gentleman." I glanced back at Mark. "We'll call it even for lunch."

Ferris took his hand away from the humidor and swept some of the coins into his hand, pouring them into the change drawer. "Pick whichever one you want, Mr. Twain."

While I took the rest of my money, Mark leaned over the humidor thoughtfully. He slipped one large, fat cigar from the humidor and then shook his head and put it back. He rejected three other cigars before he finally took the first cigar he had inspected. Ferris quickly covered the humidor with the lid and put it safely underneath the counter. "I'll be looking forward to seeing you tomorrow."

"Right." Mark held the cigar horizontally underneath his nose and sniffed it appreciatively. "I can't tell you how grateful I am, young—I mean, Your Grace." He slipped the cigar momentarily into the breast pocket of his coat, giving it a protective pat.

"What's in the envelope?" I asked.

"I suppose I ought to see." Mark took out the blue envelope and tore it open.

I leaned over far enough to see that the note was scrawled in a hasty hand. It said:

> *If you would like to learn something of interest concerning Digger and Billy's whereabouts, come alone to 453 Green Street, Room 17, before two this afternoon.*

There was no signature.

"It could be a trap," I suggested. "I think you ought to get Bulldog Brill."

Mark flipped the note back and forth over his fingertips. "He'd just call this a forgery."

"I guess Captain Purdy would say the same thing." I bit my lip thoughtfully for a moment. Funny, but now that I had saved his life, I was beginning to feel responsible for him. For all of his dress and talk, he was still like an overgrown boy. "Well, couldn't you round up some friends to go with you?"

Mark scratched the tip of his nose. "I suppose I could." But he didn't sound very excited. "It's just that I owe money to so many of them."

"It's payday tonight," I reminded him.

Mark laughed sourly. "You're overestimating the size of my salary and underestimating the size of my debts." He added gloomily, "So now you know what the name of Mark Twain is really worth in this city."

I suppose Mark was fishing for some kind of sympathy from me—the kind where you tell someone everything is going to be all right, then give them your hanky to cry in and a cup of tea to drink. But all that kind of sympathy was good for was to dirty up a lot of hankies and teacups.

"Well, what did you expect?" I said. "You've only played at being a reporter up till now. Why should they take you seriously just because you ask them to?"

"That's right"—Mark glowered at me—"drive the last nail into my coffin."

"Who said anything about rolling over and playing dead?" I waved a hand back and forth between myself and Mark. "There're two of us, aren't there? If it's a trap, we'll just turn it right around on those raiders and catch them instead."

Mark patted the pistol in his coat pocket. "You mean the three of us." He tucked the note away in his pocket. "I'll tell you what. You can stand watch outside. If I'm out by the time you count to two hundred, you go get the police."

"I'll count to a hundred," I sniffed. "I know just how much good that pistol's going to do you."

453 Green Street was a large two-story boardinghouse in the middle of a weed-grown lot with a small chicken coop in the back. It had been a long time since the house had seen a coat of paint, but otherwise it seemed pretty clean and respectable. There were curtains in every window and the panes all seemed intact—and that was a combination hard to find in that neighborhood.

Bricks had even been laid to form a path from the gate to the stairs leading up to the front door. Mark paused and slipped his right hand into his pocket where his pistol was. "Don't forget now. Count to two hundred real slow. If I'm not out by then, or if I don't signal to you that everything's all right, run for help as fast as you can."

"Hey"—I plucked at his sleeve—"did you pull back the gun hammer?"

"What?" Mark frowned as he tried to recall whether he had or not. "Tarnation, I don't think I did." He jammed his other hand into his pocket and fumbled around until there was a loud click. Then, taking a deep breath, he marched up the steps and into the house.

I started to count real slow while I kept a careful watch. I thought I saw a curtain stir in an upper window to my left but I couldn't be sure. I had just reached ninety-seven when I thought I saw Mark beckon to me from that same window.

When I entered the house, I found myself in a hallway where a narrow stairway angled upward to the next story. I paused for a moment, holding onto the banister with my free hand. The house looked much larger once I was inside. I could hear a baby crying faintly in the distance and from somewhere to the rear of the house I could hear the clanking of pots and pans as if someone was washing them.

"Mark?" I called, but there wasn't any answer.

I took the steps one by one. It seemed like a long time before I found myself on the next landing. Facing me was a hallway with at least five doors opening into rooms that looked out on the rear of the house. There was another hallway at the front of the house leading to more rooms.

"Mark?" I called again.

A door immediately opened in the front hallway and a hand waved impatiently for me to come over. The sleeve behind the hand looked like the sleeve to Mark's coat, but I couldn't be sure.

So I stayed right where I was, ready to bolt back down the stairs. "Mark, are you all right?"

Suddenly a door banged open to the right of the stairway and I whirled around to see the leather-faced Confederate step out from a closet with the Le Mat in his hand. I turned to run, but the man brought the barrels of the Le Mat crashing against my skull, and I was falling into the sudden darkness.

· CHAPTER ·
6

When I woke up, I had a lump on the back of my head the size of a walnut. I sat up slowly and blinked my eyes, forcing myself to see.

Mark lay sprawled beside me on the dirty mattress, his hands tied. He was clad only in his red union suit, and he seemed to be out cold. To my right was a large, heavy bureau on which sat a gray earthenware pitcher and washbasin. In the center of the room, underneath a hanging kerosene lamp, were two chairs—the only other pieces of furniture besides the bureau and the bed.

Our clothes lay in a heap by the bureau while a small pile of objects sat at the foot of the bed. I recognized some of the things from my pockets as well as Mark's notebook. I suppose the other items also belonged to Mark. His five-shooter wasn't there, of course. Neither was the cigar for which I had paid hard cash.

The next moment the door opened and the leather-faced man was staring at me. "Major," he called over his shoulder, "the boy's up." He came into the room, reached across Mark, and shoved me back down on the mattress. "You stay put, you little varmint."

"There's no call for that." The major, still wearing

Mark's coat, strolled into the room and smiled at me encouragingly. "We're not waging war against children." In his left hand I noticed a cigar—probably the cigar which I had bought for Mark. "What about Mr. Clemens?" He set the cigar between his teeth while he stripped off Mark's coat.

"Still out." The leather-faced man picked up the earthenware pitcher from the bureau and looked questioningly at the major.

The major nodded his head as he added Mark's coat to the pile of clothing.

The leather-faced man splashed dirty water onto Mark. He sat up spluttering, his bound hands clumsily wiping at his eyes.

While the leather-faced man set the pitcher back on the bureau, the major seated himself in one of the chairs. "Captain," he said in a soft, cultured voice, "I believe the gentleman of the fourth estate is badly in need of some headache remedy." He slipped a small silver flask from his boot.

Mark took the flask in both hands and sniffed it suspiciously. "This smells like aged Kentucky bourbon." He sniffed it again. "Where did you get this from?"

"A body needs its comforts, Mr. Clemens. Drink up." The major waved grandly to Mark.

Mark sipped from the flask and leaned over to hand it to the captain. "I haven't been called Clemens since I left Missouri." Mark scratched his forehead. "You have the advantage of me, sir." Mark glanced at the leather-faced man. "In fact, quite a few advantages."

From the relaxed way the major was sitting, you would have thought that we were in his parlor some

Sunday afternoon discussing poetry. "You must forgive my manners." The major inclined his head with elaborate courtesy. "My name is St. John. Ashley St. John." He pronounced it like Sin-Jin. "I have the honor of holding a major's commission in the Army of the Confederate States of America." He motioned to the leather-faced man. "And my associate here is Captain Jack Fletcher."

That name sounded awfully familiar to me. I wrinkled my forehead, trying to remember some of Mark's talk. Suddenly I pointed a finger at the leather-faced man. "You're the thief who's been robbing all those banks and stagecoaches."

Fletcher's mouth tightened like some Sunday-school teacher who had just heard a bad word. "The raider," he corrected me quickly. "I've got a commission from Jeff Davis hisself." His voice was dry, as if his insides were just as hard and leathery as his outside. "I didn't pocket none of the money; it was all for this operation." He took a quick gulp from the flask, then capped it and returned it to the major with a backward fling of his hand.

Then Fletcher plopped down in the other chair. He seemed like someone who was used to doing everything in a hurry, from drinking to talking.

"Treat the bourbon with a bit more respect, Captain." St. John's fingers carefully wiped the mouth of the flask before he took a sip himself. "You puzzle me, Mr. Clemens." The major capped the flask and stowed it away inside his boot again. "Why are you making things so difficult for us? After all, you once fought for the South."

"It was only in a militia company, and it was such a poor outfit that they elected me a lieutenant." Mark looked mournfully at the cigar dangling wastefully between the major's fingers. "Now how could I respect any military outfit that would have me as an officer?"

St. John smiled. "But you didn't oppose the institution of slavery?"

Mark squirmed. "Well, I didn't exactly support it, either."

"Then I think we have something in common because neither did I." St. John crossed his legs. "Like any reasonable person before the war, I could see that slavery kept the Southern economy from growing and improving." He began to wriggle his leg. "But I also knew that the South must be allowed to end slavery gradually so that the slaves might be trained and our own economy might be allowed to adjust. However, those Yankee bankers and their puppet, Mr. Lincoln, would have us cut our own throats at their command."

"That's a pretty enough speech," Mark said quietly, "but slaves are human beings, not machines."

St. John leaned forward suddenly. "So it's people you care about, is it? Then let me tell you about my family. When the war started, I found that I could fight neither for the South, nor against it." He looked grim. "Like everyone, I thought the war would be over in a month, so I closed up my bookstore and took my family to a house my wife had inherited in the Shenandoah Valley."

St. John's voice gathered a terrible kind of momentum, like a wagon rolling down a hill. "A band of Yankee horsemen came into our yard one day." St. John let his foot drop to the floor. "They killed my wife and daughter and they nearly killed me." St. John seemed to become aware that he was not in his parlor but in a bleak, almost empty room in a city far away from his home. "I stopped being a reasonable man then. I'm fighting to end this war and without that Yankee scum as our conquerors."

"It's a sad story, Major," Mark said quietly, "but I've heard stories just as sad about what Confederate raiders have done. I finally left the States just to get away from that kind of madness."

"But this is precisely the kind of war you cannot escape," St. John scolded him mildly. Spreading the fingers of one hand, he pretended to flatten a bug against a wall. "However, I can see no useful purpose in further debate. I'll put my proposition to you plainly. You've become something of a thorn in our side; but even so, we bear you no ill will. You won't be harmed if you give me your word that you'll cooperate with us and not try to escape for the next few days." The major was, perhaps, too friendly . . . too eager.

Mark asked suspiciously, "Cooperate in what way?"

"Nothing compromising." The major held up a reassuring hand. "Merely a trifle. But first"—with a lazy smile he flicked the ash from his cigar tip—"your word as a gentleman."

"Well, what do you think, Your Grace?" Mark asked me.

"Your Grace?" The major gave me a quizzical smile.

"The Duke of Baywater." I inclined my head to him.

"It must be Johnny's son," Fletcher muttered to the major.

"Of course," the major laughed. "So what do you say,

Mr. Clemens? It's even to your advantage because you'd have the exclusive inside story."

"I was talking to my partner," Mark frowned, "before you interrupted."

"Partner?" The major pointed at me. "The boy's crazy as a loon."

I looked at the major. He dressed and spoke so nicely and had such elaborate manners that I would have sworn he was the first genuine gentleman I had met. But the major's fancy talk and dress and manners were only the elegant wrappings around a heart as hard as Johnny Dougherty's.

Mark shifted his legs and sniffed. "I'd like to see you come out half as well, Major, being raised the way he was."

"Come now, Mr. Clemens, will you agree to my proposition?" the major asked in the lazy, confident tone of people who are used to having things go exactly the way they want.

"Well?" Mark nudged me.

"I don't trust him," I said simply—not that I thought my vote would count much with Mark. I knew he was going to accept the major's offer. After all, Mark was not the bravest of souls.

"You know, Major, no one takes me very seriously in this city. Not you. Not my friends. Not even my editor. I suppose I didn't even take myself very seriously until I met the Duke of Baywater here." Mark heaved his shoulders up and down in a massive shrug. "But if I learned anything from him, it's that even the laziest reporter in San Francisco ought to have some pride."

My jaw dropped open as I stared at Mark. He winked

at me. Well, he might not have been the most dependable person in the world and he might have dressed a bit too flashily, but he was more of a gentleman at that moment than the major ever would be.

For his part, the major had been just as surprised as me. He sat up straight, blinking his eyes. "You're sure?" Mark rested his head on the bed's lumpy pillow. "More or less."

"I'm truly sorry then," St. John said, in a flat, almost mechanical voice. "Will you dispose of them, Captain? Better not use a gun, though. We wouldn't want to disturb the neighbors."

"Wait a moment," I said angrily. "You can't order people's deaths like . . . "—I struggled for the right words— ". . . like you were giving your shopping list to the grocer."

"Which of us is the worse sinner: your General Grant or myself?" St. John rose indignantly from his chair. "I deal in one death at a time and I know each victim personally. Grant impersonally ordered thousands of men to their death in a matter of minutes at the battle of Cold Harbor." St. John paused and then shook his head in puzzlement. He still did not understand why I might resent the fact that he had ordered our deaths.

I realized right then that the major was not a true gentleman. He was polite to people because it was expected of him—like polishing his boots to a bright shine. But a gentleman, I decided, ought to be a gentle person. He ought to care about other people just like Mark had said yesterday. The funny thing is that St. John could probably fool most people into thinking he was more of a gentleman than Mark was.

I was going to argue some more, but the major seemed bored now with the whole conversation. "I'll be outside, Captain."

The major strode across the floor and shut the door behind him with all the finality of a coffin lid. Fletcher pulled a wicked-looking knife from his boot and gave us an anxious, apologetic smile. "I'll make it real quick. You won't feel a thing."

Mark licked his lips nervously. "Mind if I put on my pants first?"

He was stalling for time and Fletcher knew it. But I guess he figured that it didn't matter, because he nodded his head finally. "Sure, I figure a person ought to die with a little dignity." As a precaution, he took out the Le Mat, cocked it, and pointed it at Mark. "But be careful. Don't try nothing."

"I'm going to be missed, you know." Mark sorted through the pile of clothing.

Laughing, Fletcher rocked back in his chair. "You ain't exactly Mr. Reliability. Nobody's going to be looking for you tonight; and by tomorrow night we're off." Mark glanced at me. At least we knew the time limit for their plot.

"For what? Do you have a secret army that's going to attack?" Mark held his pants open so he could slip one leg in. "Was the *Haze* bringing guns to them?"

Fletcher jerked his head in delight. "Don't need an army, Clemens. All we had to do was to make the Yankees think we did so's they'd move most of their troops out of San Francisco."

"Are you going to blow up the *Camanche?*" Mark almost lost his balance as he thrust his other leg into his pants. "Is that what St. John wanted from me? Details about the shipyard?" I suppose that, as a reporter, Mark had been there a lot of times.

"I told you all I'm going to." Fletcher tipped his chair back on its two rear legs and then righted it again. "But the major's got something real big planned. And slick? I hope to tell you." He shook his head in admiration for St. John. "By the time we're finished, Lincoln will be out on his backside and the Peace Democrats are going to be walking through the White House door."

Mark pulled his pants up to his waist. "How do you figure that?"

"This war ain't all that popular back in the North." Fletcher stretched his legs. "Folks been rioting against the draft."

"I know. Just a year ago, they had over fifty thousand people rioting in New York." Mark started to jam his feet into his shoes. "I hear they caused a million and a half dollars' worth of damage."

"Folks are down right *sick* of the war," Fletcher instructed Mark. "It would take just one more incident to make people throw Lincoln out of office."

Since I didn't have my hands tied like Mark, I managed to put on my shirt as well as my trousers. With my hat on my head and my shoes and stockings in my hand, I sat on the bed. "Did you sink that ship carrying the *Camanche*'s parts?"

"We weren't even here then," he said, as he swung the pistol toward me, "but we weren't too unhappy to hear about it."

"No, I bet you weren't." I quickly pulled my stockings on over my feet.

Keeping an eye on Mark and me, Fletcher leaned forward to stir the knife through the small pile of things on the mattress. "Say, boy, where's Pettibone's coin?"

I hardly dared to breathe when I saw Fletcher's gun waver and then drop slightly. "You mean Felix is still working for you?" I crossed my legs and tugged a shoe over one foot. I watched the Confederate carefully.

"The man's loyal to whoever pays him the most." Fletcher shoved the change around some more. "But he does like to have what's his, and I like to keep my boys happy. So where's the coin?"

His gun dropped another inch.

I figured that if they hadn't found the penny in my pocket, it was probably lying in Ferris's cash drawer at the cigar stand of the Occidental Hotel; but I was not about to tell Fletcher that. "It could be a lot of places." I recrossed my legs as if to put on the other shoe. "Mark had me spending money all over the city."

"Like where?" Fletcher's gun dipped even lower.

With a desperate snap of my wrist, I flung my shoe at Fletcher's head.

"Tarnation." Ducking, Fletcher started to bring up his gun again. But in the meantime, my left hand had found the pillow. I whipped it toward Fletcher as I dove for the floor.

There was a muffled roar and part of the pillow disintegrated, sending a cloud of singed feathers whirling around the room.

Coughing from the smell of burning feathers, Fletcher had thrown off what was left of the pillow and cocked his gun again. Too late, he saw Mark looming over him with the pitcher grasped in both hands. Fletcher started to spin around just as the pitcher broke into a half-dozen large chunks against his head. With a groan, he slumped to the floor.

Mark held out his wrists to me. "Cut me loose, will you?"

I got hold of Fletcher's knife and sliced through the rope. "I've just about had my fill of Southern hospitality, haven't you?"

"It can be a little tiresome." Mark dragged the Le Mat from the Confederate's hand just as the door burst open.

St. John stood there with a razor in his right hand, lather covering part of his chin. He was wearing the blue pants of a Yankee soldier. "What the—"

His eyes widened as Mark jerked up the Le Mat, which had already been cocked by Fletcher. Mark did not hesitate this time. St. John dove for cover as the shot splintered the doorway.

Mark looked down at the Le Mat. "I wonder how in the devil you fire the lower barrel."

"We can ask Fletcher that when he's behind bars." I found my other shoe and put it on.

We heard a door open in the other room and St. John began to shout. "He shot my friend. He just up and shot him."

By the time Mark had reached the bedroom door, St. John was already on the landing surrounded by a crowd of curious people. "That's the man." St. John pointed at Mark. "He killed my friend."

"Now you ought to hear my side first. For one thing, the man's unconscious, not dead. For another thing, they're Confederate spies." To show his good intentions, Mark started to raise the pistol over his head. Immediately a heavy-set man charged through the doorway and pinned Mark to the floor. Two more men tumbled into the room and snatched the gun from Mark's hand.

"I didn't kill anyone," Mark kept shouting. But the heavy-set man only folded his arms as he sat down on Mark's chest.

They were all busy with Mark so I dropped the knife and slipped out the door and into the crowd. St. John was already gone.

It was nearly three o'clock when I walked up to the bars of Mark's jail cell. "What are you doing here?" Mark asked.

"Is that the way to talk to your brother?" I winked at him.

Mark began shuffling the papers on his lap. "As if my family didn't have enough trouble with me tarnishing its reputation."

When the turnkey opened the cell door, I stepped inside. "Have you been writing?"

Mark tucked the pencil stub away in his pocket. "There wasn't anything else to do so I borrowed some paper to work on my stories. Not a bad place to work, really." He handed one sheet to me as I sat down. It contained the story of our kidnapping and his false arrest, told with a good deal of ginger and fire. Mark could certainly write when he'd a mind to.

Footsteps again echoed in the corridor. "Hello, Bull-dog," Mark called as the detective strode up to the cell.

"You've really gone and done it this time." Bulldog Brill shook his head.

"Now wait." Mark took his article back from me. "I

caught that raider, Fletcher. He'll tell you the truth. . . ."
Mark's voice faltered as he saw the expression on
Bulldog's face.

"All I know is that you were found in a room being
guarded by a dozen people who said you had tried to kill
a man." Bulldog consulted the report in his hand. "A
Mr. Elmer Bristol of San Jose. He claims you broke into
his place with some wild story, then hit him on the head
when he protested." Bulldog pointed the report at Mark.
"You're going to be sued for criminal trespass, assault,
and I don't know what else. I'll find out when Bristol's
lawyer finishes consulting with Peever."

"Not Peever." Mark could not help moaning.

"That's right," Bulldog said grimly. "He's going to
settle some old scores with you."

"Well," I rose hurriedly, "it's been nice talking to you,
Mark."

Bulldog pointed a finger at me. "You stay right there.
The report also has some talk of a short accomplice."

"Maybe I can talk to that lawyer." Mark rested his
head against his hands for a moment. "What's his
name?"

"Meredith, a new fellow from Baltimore." Bulldog
rolled the report into a cylinder. "But awfully soft-
spoken for a lawyer."

Mark rose from his cot. "What does he look like?
Thin? Blond? Blue eyes?"

Bulldog's eyes flicked toward Mark. "Yeah. Have you
met him before?"

"He sounds like the head Confederate, Major St.
John." Mark clung to the bars of his cell. "You better
check on this Meredith. If he's got any identification,

you can bet it's forged. Get hold of Judge Shepherd. He's on the local bar association. The judge ought to know this fellow if he's practicing law."

"This had better check out." Bulldog scowled.

Mark pressed his face against the bars. "And for heaven's sake, don't let Meredith out of the building."

It was a long, hellish hour before a humble Bulldog returned with the turnkey who opened the door. "All right, Mark." Bulldog waved him out of the cell.

Mark straightened, trying to dust off his dirty coat and pants. "What did Meredith say?" he asked eagerly.

"Meredith, or whoever he is, was gone by the time I finished talking to Judge Shepherd." Bulldog ran an embarrassed hand over his chin. "But I'll keep on his trail until I catch him. In the meantime, we're putting the clamps on this little fandango. No one's going to know."

"What about the charges against me?" Mark stepped out of the cell and stretched.

"Being put into a drawer until we can find either that Bristol—or Fletcher or whatever his name is." He held out a small box which held Mark's things.

Mark couldn't help sounding annoyed. "You mean Fletcher's gone, too?"

"We don't hold the victim of the crime," Bulldog shrugged.

"Usually," Mark grimaced. "Well, do you believe me now?" He picked up his hat.

Bulldog, however, was unrepentant. "I'll believe that you're in with a pretty slippery crowd, Mark," was the only concession that Bulldog seemed willing to make. "What do you have to prove that they're spies? Only their word, right?"

"But I saw St. John with a Yankee uniform on," Mark protested. "Ask the people in that boardinghouse."

Bulldog ushered Mark through the iron door into the police station. "Monday, Mark."

"No," Mark insisted, "you've got to interrogate Felix Pettibone right now."

"Monday," Bulldog repeated.

"Monday will be too late." He grabbed Bulldog's lapel. "Damn it, Bulldog, those Rebs are going to try to blow up the *Camanche*."

Bulldog impatiently took Mark's arm. "Right, Mark. Now let me give you an escort as far as the front door."

Mark tried to dig his heels into the floor. "But Bulldog, the *Camanche* is the only real defense San Francisco is likely to have." He pointed behind us. "Somewhere out on that ocean there could be a Confederate privateer. I hear the *Florida*'s still operating. She's sunk or taken easily a million dollars' worth of shipping. If she comes into the bay," Mark shook his head, "well, I don't know anything to stop it."

Bulldog shrugged fatalistically. "If what you say is true, you'll have the last laugh on everyone, myself included."

· CHAPTER ·
7

When we reached the street, we could feel a cold, damp breeze blowing through the city. It picked up the dust that lay in patches where the street planks had worn away and blew the dust into our noses and ears and under our collars. The breeze made the streets feel mean and cold and hard.

"You said people ought to care about one another"—I looked accusingly at Mark—"but no one seems to care what happened to us."

Mark sighed. "Your trouble is the company you keep." He tucked his pencil behind his ear. "If the warning had come from any other reporter but me, the police and the army would have begun checking by now." He patted his left lapel. "But when I publish the story of our kidnapping, every soldier and policeman in this city will hang his head in shame."

"And in the meantime, what about the major?"

"Where are we going to find him?" Mark shrugged. "I can't spend the whole day trying to track him down. I've got my beat to cover."

Though Mark did not mention the Confederates for the rest of the day, it was plain to see that they still occupied his mind. He was more impatient than usual with people and he would not talk to me much.

Even when we went to the Occidental for a late supper, Mark did not forget the Confederates. Once we were in the lobby, he walked right to the cigar stand. Like me, he had figured that Felix's penny was there. But a little sign said that Ferris had gone home sick for the evening.

Mark drummed his fingers on the counter top. "I wonder why Fletcher wanted that coin?"

After we had shared the same supper plate, Mark made his round of the theaters. He walked along cautiously, but there was not so much as a hint of our Confederate friends. They were probably too busy to be bothered with us now.

When Mark arrived at the *Call*, his editor growled that he was late again. "But this time I've already got my articles written up." Mark waved the handful of stories he had done while waiting in the cell.

Barnes took his cigar from his mouth and scratched his chin real hard like a dog trying to kill a pesky flea. "What did you find out about the *Haze?*"

"Well, for one thing, they caught some man on board the *Haze* that had been on the *Chapman*." Mark took the first story from his bunch of papers and laid it in front of Barnes with a mock bow. "There, O Prince, is the first gem."

Barnes squinted at the story for a moment and then waved his hand disgustedly at it. "I always have a hard time reading your infernal scrawl, but this is worse than usual. What does it say?"

Rapidly Mark filled Barnes in on his interview with

Lieutenant Bainbridge. Barnes said nothing while Mark spoke, but he began puffing excitedly at his cigar until he resembled a locomotive getting up steam. When Mark stopped talking, Barnes snatched his cigar from his mouth. "Have you got a definite quote from the lieutenant?"

Mark's collar suddenly seemed to feel very tight. He ran a finger under it. "I'm afraid not," Mark had to confess. "He not only said he'd deny it, but even threatened to arrest me for trying to incite a riot if I tried to suggest it."

About an inch of ash spilled across Barnes's lap. He swiped at it disgustedly and wound up only smearing the ash over a wider area. He turned to the other writer. "Frank, maybe you better take this story then."

Mark clutched his sheaf of stories. "Quit treating me like Frank's legman. I went out and got facts just like you said to do." Mark began to fan himself with his stories. "Even without that part about the Confederates, I've still got enough facts to make a good story about the *Haze* itself."

Barnes slowly ground his cigar out on the plate, choosing each of his words carefully. "Mark, it's just that . . . "—he sighed—"it's just that the gravity of this matter might not be suited to your style."

"Y-a-a-s, well, I almost got myself killed today getting this next story." Triumphantly Mark went through the bunch of papers and slapped one down on Barnes's desk. "That ought to prove to you how serious I am."

"I can't read this one either. What happened?"

Mark stood motionless for a moment, his lips moving as he counted to ten before he trusted himself to speak.

"These Confederate raiders tried to kidnap me and His Grace after lunch."

Over at his place, Frank broke into a laugh.

Mark whirled. "It's true." He turned back to Barnes. "I swear it's true." He gestured toward the story. "I put it all down just like it happened. I'm not about to risk losing this job by coming up with another hoax."

Barnes pressed his fingertips together. "You've talked to the police?"

Mark swallowed. "And the military. Neither of them would believe me, but. . . ."

Barnes picked up the story of our kidnapping and slowly, deliberately crumpled it into a small ball. "Recopy your other stories before I read them." He raised his hand to throw the story away.

Mark caught his wrist. "Now hold on, Barnes. Baywater and I risked our lives today to get this story." He nodded his head to me insistently. "Ask His Grace."

Barnes made no answer. He stared uncomfortably at Mark, as if he wished Mark were far away from him at this moment.

Mark let go of Barnes's wrist. "You've got to believe me," Mark pleaded. "I could have agreed to do what those Confederates wanted or at least lied to them to save our necks." Mark flattened his own palm against his chest. "But I wouldn't. I'm serious about this writing business."

"Mark," Barnes sighed, "you've backed me into a corner, so there's no graceful way of putting this." He rubbed his pink, bald head. "But we only have the word of yourself and a crazy boy for all of this poppycock, right?"

"The police are covering it up because I was falsely arrested." Mark slammed a fist on the desk top. "But I swear to you that I didn't make it up."

"Well, your word isn't good enough," Barnes said quietly.

Mark straightened. He glanced at the rest of his stories as if he would have liked to crumple them up as well. He raised his shoulders as he took a deep, long breath. "It's a fine thing to find out that you have integrity and no one else values it."

Barnes chucked the story into a corner of the office as far away from himself as possible. "I don't mean to bullyrag you, Mark, but you've played the clown most of your life. You've run up debts with half the city. And suddenly you expect me to treat you like a respectable, hardworking citizen—just because you ask me to?" Barnes tipped his head back. "Now no one respects your talents more than I do; but far be it from me to hold you back if you want to quit."

Mark was a sorry sight. He just stood there with his shoulders sagging and his head hung down. I suppose he was thinking of all of his bad debts. "Y-a-a-s, well"— Mark adjusted the visor of his eyeshade—"I reckon I'll give you a hand for a little while longer."

"I thought you'd see things my way." Contemptuously Barnes turned away from Mark. "Recopy the rest of your stories so I can read them, and if any of them have a hint of your fanciful embroidery, you'll have your liberty whether you want it or not."

Mark began to twist the stories between his two hands as if he would have liked to tear them up right then and simply turn his back on the newspaper. But he could not afford to quit that night any more than the night before.

"I'll be waiting outside," I whispered.

Mark was too embarrassed to look at even me. Barnes had managed to shred what little dignity and self-respect Mark had left. "I'll pay you the full amount," he snapped. "Don't worry."

I had not been thinking about the money at all, but about Mark. Still, I could not see what good it would do to tell him that right then. I went outside to sit on the landing, leaning my head against the railing while I tried to nap. But every now and then I would lift my head when I thought I heard the sound of an explosion. I found myself almost wishing there would be one.

It was not until two o'clock or so that Mark left the office. He jingled the coins in a small tan envelope. "Well, Your Grace, here's your money." He slid some of the coins from the envelope into the palm of his other hand and counted out two silver dollars, a dime, two pennies and a half cent. "I hope it's been entertaining, if not educational."

I had begun to like Mark in the day and a half that I had known him, so I did not like what I saw happening. "Mark, are you just going to lie in the dirt and let all these folks step on you?"

Mark was silent for a moment as Frank passed by. He waited until Frank was on the next flight of stairs before he would answer in a low voice that cracked with anger. "I say let Bulldog and Purdy and Barnes and the whole city stew in their own juices. I'm going to let St. John blow up the *Camanche*," he said. "And then just you wait and read the stories that I'll write. I'll make everyone sorry that they ignored us," he added confidently.

"And I'll make a big name for myself at the same time."

I just stared at the coins in Mark's hand. I had never been fussy before about where my money came from; but then, I had never much cared about the people who were paying me. Only this was different. "I expected better things from you, Mark."

Mark squatted down and slapped the coins on the floor beside me. "And just what do you think we can do against the major and his gang? If we went there, we'd be caught and blown up along with the *Camanche*."

I picked up the coins one by one and put them away. "At least we ought to try and do something."

Straightening up, Mark emptied the rest of the coins from his pay envelope and put them into his pocket and then flipped the envelope away. "What's gotten into you? Do you want revenge for Johnny? Is that it?"

"It's not revenge." I grabbed hold of the stair railing and pulled myself up to my feet. With my toe I drew an imaginary line across the wooden landing—as if daring Mark to step across. "It's going to stick in my craw if I just sit and let the major wreck the city and then go around later telling everyone, 'I told you so.'"

Mark opened his mouth but shut it grimly as if his answer did not sit well with him. He tried opening his mouth again but again closed it as if his second answer did not feel any better than the first. Finally, he took a long, deep breath and let it out slowly. "Y-a-a-s, well, I suppose you ought to be able to say that about anybody worth their salt." Mark scratched one of his bushy eyebrows and glared at me. "You're a pest, you know that?" He grinned crookedly. "And the worst thing of all is that you've usually been right."

He passed by me and started down the stairs. "What are you waiting for?" He looked over his shoulder.

"You mean you're going along?"

Mark drummed his fingers on the stair railing. "I've been a riverboat pilot and a miner and a businessman, and I don't think I've ever finished anything I ever started out to do." He gripped the railing and gave himself a shove down the steps. "Maybe this will be the first time I'll do something right." His voice echoed up the stairs. "And maybe it'll be the last time, too."

It was close to two-thirty in the morning when we reached Steamboat Point where the *Camanche* was being reassembled. To the north lay the lights of the brick Marine Hospital at Rincon Point. Between the two points lay a fleet of ships moored at the wharves or resting on the ways of the shipyards. There were tall-masted sailing ships and steamships with stubby funnels; sleek ocean vessels and squat riverboats and tugs. The bay at that moment looked so peaceful and helpless, but I could easily imagine a fire sweeping through the shipyards and on up the wharves into the city.

The shipyard with the *Camanche* lay on a beach below the point. "I'm sorry, sir." The sentry held his rifle at port arms. "But please keep your distance from the gate."

Mark stared hard at the sentry, but he didn't look like Felix or either of the Confederates. "Everything all right?"

"Just fine, sir. Now move on." The sentry's knuckles tightened around the rifle.

"Don't get trigger-happy." Mark turned to the right. "See, I'm moving on." He walked on for only another hundred yards before he stopped at the gate to the next shipyard. The watchman clumped slowly up the path with a lantern in one hand and a shotgun in the other. He peered through the slats of the gate. "Mr. Twain, what are you doing here?" He spoke with a slight Norwegian accent. "I'd lend you what I could, but the missus gets everything in my pay envelope."

"I didn't come down here for money, Oscar." Mark crooked a finger through the gate slats; and when Oscar had leaned forward, Mark whispered into his ear, "I think the Confederates might try to raid your neighbors tonight so I came down to help."

Oscar straightened with a wink. "I got you, Mr. Twain. You been thrown out of your rooming house again. Well, you're welcome to sleep here tonight."

By now, Mark seemed to know better than to fight his reputation. "I'd appreciate it, Oscar." He turned and motioned to me. "I brought a friend along, the Duke of Baywater. He doesn't have any place to stay either." As Oscar began to frown, Mark hastily ad-libbed. "He's a great checkers player."

"Oh, well, that's different." Oscar unlocked the gate and swung it open. "Don't usually get much company down here. We can have a regular tournament tonight."

We followed Oscar down the path that wound across the slope of the point to the beach. Mark and I had difficulty making our way across the splintered boards, bent rusty bolts and discarded lengths of cable. Oscar, however, moved almost instinctively, clambering over a barrel here, hopping over broken timbers there until he reached the shipyard office, a small wooden building which lay against the slope.

Through the rickety fence separating the two ship-yards, Mark could see the sentry walking his rounds in the disorder of the *Camanche's* shipyard. Beyond the sentry was the *Camanche.* She lay on the greased ways like the skeleton of a beached whale. Heavy beams, reinforced with iron, formed the keel, a hundred and sixty feet long from stem to sternpost with two hundred feet for her deck on which her revolving turret would turn. It was a long, slow painful process to replace the items that had been broken in the wreck or that still remained in the bay. Iron plates were scattered in heaps on either side, some of them with numbers chalked upon their rusting sides, waiting to be used.

"I thought"—Mark scratched his head ruefully—"there might be more to blow up since the last time I saw her."

Oscar hung his lantern on a nail by the door. "Well, a barrel of kerosene and a match'd do more damage at this stage." He turned the doorknob. "Want to play the first game, Mr. Twain?"

Mark stepped down off the office porch. "Actually, I think I'd like to take in the view for a while." I just hoped that none of the sentries would get nervous at having him as their next-door neighbor.

Oscar gave him a puzzled smile. "Suit yourself," he said, and motioned me inside. "This way, boy."

"Your Grace," I corrected him. Through the open doorway, I could see Mark rummage through a pile of scrap lumber until he found a section of two-by-four to use as a club. It wouldn't be much against pistols, but I suppose Mark thought he needed something. Then he sat down on the sand with his back against an overturned rowboat, slapping every now and then at the mosquitoes. To his right, the scummy green water sucked at the lower timbers of the way. To his left, the lights of the city gleamed.

Mark nervously began to pound one of the two-by-fours against the sand. "Come on, St. John," he growled. "Come on."

· CHAPTER ·
8

We were both pretty tired and aching when we limped into the Occidental Hotel the next morning. "Well, I guess we were wrong about their target being the *Camanche*." Scratching his mosquito bites, Mark said to me, "You must think me the biggest fool in the city."

"Not the biggest. After all, it was my idea in the first place to go down there." I stifled a yawn with my hand. "But Oscar sure likes to play checkers, doesn't he?" We'd stayed up most of the night holding a checkers tournament. As long as one of Oscar's kings could pull off a triple jump, he wouldn't have cared if San Francisco had slid into the ocean.

"I should have warned you." Mark cupped a hand behind his ear. "Listen to that music, will you?" The clatter of forks and knives on plates could be heard coming from the dining room. "I didn't realize just how hungry I was."

We had started for the dining room when Mark caught sight of Ferris back at his cigar stand. "Just a moment. It's only a small chance, but maybe that penny is really a clue to the major's plans."

"I thought you were going to give up on it," I said.

"If something's worth doing, it's worth doing well."
Mark grinned back at me. "Morning, Ferris," he called
as he strode up to the stand.

"Good morning, Mr. Twain." Ferris checked to make
sure the humidor was beyond Mark's reach.

Mark slapped his hand down on top of the counter.
"Did you happen to find a brass penny the other day?"

"So you're the one who gave it to me." Ferris reached
his hand into his pants pocket and slipped the coin onto
the glass counter top. "When I was counting through the
change yesterday, I thought it was counterfeit."

"Funny coin, isn't it?" Mark put another penny onto
the stand to exchange for it. "It's one of the new ones."

"Is that a fact?" Ferris picked up the other coin,
rubbing his fingers across its surface. "I think I like the
old ones better."

Mark stowed the penny safely away in his pocket. "I
know, a penny ought to have a copper look and feel to
it."

"By the way." Ferris snapped his fingers. "You were
paid last night, weren't you, Mr. Twain?"

"Right. I'll get back to you later." Mark and I beat a
hasty retreat into the dining room. We got a lot of looks
when we entered there, I suppose because Mark hadn't
changed since yesterday. Mark, though, didn't seem to
notice. He kept turning the penny over and over in his
fingers all through breakfast as if trying to figure out the
puzzle.

"It's no use," he frowned. "I'll just have to talk with
Harte."

"Who's Harte?" I lifted a large piece of omelette on my
fork and thrust it into my mouth.

"Bret Harte." Mark clenched his hand around the penny and put it away. "He's the self-proclaimed ringleader of San Francisco's literary mob. The Superintendent of the Mint hired him as his secretary. Pretty cushy job because Harte doesn't have to do much and he can concentrate on his stories instead." The envy was plain in Mark's voice as he used his fork to cut off part of his own omelette.

"Mark," I said, "the Mint begins with an *M.*"

Mark slowly lowered his fork. "That's got to be it." He slid his chair back with a loud scraping sound. "Let's go."

"But I'm not finished."

"If this works out"—Mark jerked me out of my chair—"I'll buy you dinner in the most expensive restaurant in San Francisco."

The church bells were beginning to ring all over the city for Sunday services as we headed toward Bret Harte's home, which lay within a fashionable district of San Francisco. He lived in a nice, if not fancy, frame house with a small ornamental fence protecting the garden. It was quite a contrast to Mark's messy little room, and I was even more impressed when a maid answered the door and led us to "Master" Harte's study.

A thick Persian rug covered the floor and books filled the shelves, which ran from the floor to the ceiling of three walls of the room. A large mahogany desk sat before the windows with a good view of the garden. On the desk itself was a stack of foolscap, various pens, and a bottle of expensive ink. Mark smiled with what seemed like malicious pleasure when he saw that all the sheets of paper were a blank white, though there were several crumpled balls of paper on the floor.

Sitting at the desk was a small man with big whiskers that swung away from his upper lip to merge with his sideburns. Even so, I could still see the weaselish lines of his face when he turned around. "Twain." He glanced at me. "And friend."

"This is the Duke of Baywater." Mark tapped me on the shoulder. "Hope we're not disturbing you."

"Not at all." He rested one arm on the back of his chair. "But what happened to you? You look like a mess." Harte himself was dressed in a blue-velvet smoking jacket with quilted red cuffs and a collar. On his head was a tasseled Turkish cap of black velvet embroidered with flowers.

"It's what happens when you sleep on the beach." Mark self-consciously brushed his sleeve.

"Money troubles, is it?" Harte got up from the chair. "Well, you'll get the knack of selling stories one of these days." He smiled cynically as his hand began to pantomime priming a water pump. "You've just got to learn how to pump those tears out of your readers."

I could see right away that Mark was not all that comfortable with Harte; but he had to be polite because Harte was the more famous writer right then. Even so, I don't think the two of them would have gotten along. For all of his joking and for all of his showing off, Mark was really a quiet, polite man. He was a soft artist's brush while Harte was a stiff, fancy hairbrush.

Mark took the penny from his pocket and handed it to Harte. "Actually, I came by to see what you know about this."

"It's one of the new ones." Harte took the penny and

stepped over to a large window to examine the coin in the bright sunlight. He frowned suddenly. "Where did you get this?"

"It was found in a rooming house on Telegraph Hill." Mark stepped up behind him.

"Telegraph Hill?" Harte closed his fist around the penny. "This shouldn't be in circulation." He held up the coin so he could point at a tiny *L* near the Indian's head. "The *L* stands for Longacre, the coin's engraver. Most of the new pennies don't have this letter because it's part of a special run that's not supposed to be released out here until the end of the year." Harte handed the coin to Mark.

"There's a soldier who claims it's his; but how could he have gotten hold of it?" Mark studied the penny himself.

"It's easy enough." Harte folded his arms. "Some of the soldiers from Black Point pull guard duty at the Mint. One of them could have stolen it from the office. There are plenty of collectors who'd pay for it."

"So the soldiers pull guard duty?" Clenching his fist around the coin, Mark punched Harte on the arm. "That's it, then. That's why the major was wearing a uniform!"

Harte stepped beyond Mark's reach. "Do you feel all right?"

"Never better." Mark tossed the penny to me and I tucked it away. "I think the Mint's going to be robbed by the Confederates."

"What?" Harte took another cautious step back.

"I know it sounds crazy, but it's true." Mark wrote 113 Virginia on a piece of paper on the desk. "Here's Bulldog Brill's home address. Tell him just what you told me about the penny and the soldiers. Make sure that he brings every available man to the Mint."

Harte, however, still seemed afraid of Mark. "This isn't some kind of joke, is it?"

"The penny's my proof." Mark crossed his arms and smiled smugly. "It's your business if you don't want to believe me; but you're going to be mighty embarrassed come Monday when you find your place cleared out."

I jerked the door open and stepped into the hallway to wait for Mark; but on his way to the door, Mark paused. "In the meantime, I'm going to the Mint." He snatched up a heavy hickory cane from where it leaned against the wall. "You don't mind if I borrow this, do you?" He was out the door before Harte could make any objection.

As we hurried to the Mint, Mark had time to think out loud. "St. John must have been really angry when Felix told him that you had the coin and that you were with me. There was too much of a chance that I might have shown the new coin to Harte and tipped everyone off."

"That's why St. John set up that ambush, to get the coin or at least get us out of the way." With a shiver, I realized something then. "We would have been killed even if you had promised to cooperate with them."

Mark grimly tightened his grip on the cane. "The major must have had most of the night to take the gold from the Mint. They might already be gone." He lengthened his stride.

Mark seemed almost relieved when he found the two drays outside the Mint. The large-hooved draft horses stood tired and sweaty in their harnesses. Mark turned me toward the *Call* Building. "They should be distributing the Sunday papers. We ought to find some help there."

"What are you doing here?" an angry voice demanded. Felix Pettibone rose from the back of the furthest dray. When he saw Felix lift up his rifle, Mark pulled me into the street behind the closer dray. "Hey," Felix shouted toward the Mint, "it's the Duke and that reporter fellow." From inside the building, I could hear other voices. Scrambling on all fours, Mark and I made our way under the dray.

With an oath, Felix jumped to the sidewalk and walked slowly toward our dray. Mark put one hand to my shoulder to keep me still. "Go when I tell you," he whispered to me. Then, lying on his side, Mark raised the cane and waited tensely as Felix drew even with the dray's horse. Then he was by the right front wheel.

"Come on out," he growled, "or I'll shoot." He began to crouch so he could aim his rifle.

With a sudden lunge, Mark stretched his arm from underneath the dray and whipped the cane as hard as he could against Felix's ankle. Felix's leg gave out, and with an angry yell he sat down hard.

Crablike, I scuttled sideways out from underneath the dray. Mark followed me a second later. I swung my body up over the side of the dray and tumbled into the back where I found six sacks of gold coins. One of the bags had been untied. It wouldn't have surprised me at all if Felix had been trying to slip a coin or two out of each bag. I started for the wagon seat but Mark beat me to it.

As he released the brake, I wheeled around in time to see Felix trying to pull himself up beside me. It was a pleasure to put my foot into Felix's face and tumble him backward onto the sidewalk.

"Hold on," Mark called. He had picked up the reins in his hands.

Suddenly Fletcher appeared in the doorway of the Mint, wearing a soldier's uniform. Mark cracked the reins across the horses' rumps. "Giddyap," he called. Fletcher aimed his rifle at me and fired. As the dray lurched forward, I fell against the sacks. The heavy lead ball thunked solidly against the wood of the dray.

Draft horses are not bred for speed, but between Fletcher's rifle shot and Mark's use of the reins, the horses decided that they had urgent business elsewhere— much to our delight.

As the wagon lumbered down the street, I pulled myself up and thoughtfully fingered the large splintered hole near the top of the dray's side. An inch higher and it would have gone into me instead.

Things might have gone all right, but then our horses seemed to grow tired after their sudden burst of speed. They slowed to a snail's pace and no amount of urging from Mark would make them move any faster. Mark glanced in back of us. Fletcher and a limping Felix had appeared three blocks behind with rifles in hand. "I don't know if we can outrun them," Mark said worriedly.

A block ahead of us I could see a middling-sized crowd, either people finishing the adventures of last evening or people getting an early start on today's. "I've got a plan," Mark said, and began hauling back on the reins, shouting, "Whoa, now, whoa." When the horses halted, Mark set the brake.

Then Mark rose to his feet. "Listen to this," he said. Putting both hands around the sides of his mouth as a partial funnel, he let out the loudest hog call I'd ever heard—and I'd heard some loud ones because there were still a few farms around the city. Ahead of him people looked up, startled. "Hey, anyone who wants to make money, come over here." Mark waved his hand urgently over his head.

A dozen tough-looking men began angling toward us. Mark pointed toward the pursuing Fletcher and Felix. "Get those two soldiers and it's a double eagle for each of you."

"Let's see the money first," said a man in a sailor's cap. He was a large, heavy-set man with a pouchy, chipmunk face.

Mark motioned to me, and I reached into the open bag to hold up a handful of coins. "Is this enough?" Mark asked.

"Mister," said the man in the sailor's cap, "consider them dead and floating in the bay." He pulled out a large dragoon from his holster. Eleven other pistols of various calibers also appeared.

Behind us, Fletcher and Felix came to a halt as the armed men gathered about Mark. Mark waved his arm grandly. "I'm making you all honorary members of the Marion Rangers," he announced to them with kingly largess. "And bonuses for everyone if you take them alive."

The horses started when the newly made Rangers began to fire; but by then Mark had the reins safely in his hands and fought to keep the nervous horses from bolting. Dropping the coins, I joined him on the seat and added my strength to holding back the horses. But as we struggled with the reins, we could not help looking behind us to see that Fletcher and Felix were dodging and darting back up the street. The other dray had appeared at the opposite intersection. It was too far to see at this distance, but it was most likely St. John in the seat of the dray. Standing behind him were two more men, probably local Confederates.

Mark let go of the reins when the horses seemed calmer. Standing up, Mark let out a whoop. "Let's go after them, boys." Ulysses S. Grant, in his finest moments, could not have sounded prouder.

But the man in the sailor's cap had turned to peer over the dray's side at the gold coins which had spilled from the sack. His lips moved as he began counting them all. His free hand tapped the arm of his neighbor. Soon the fire slackened off and the men began to circle the dray.

"Uh, let's go, boys," Mark said—more uncertainly now.

"Hey, look at this," the man in the sailor's cap called to the others. "He must have robbed a bank."

"A mint, to be precise," Mark explained. "Now about those others. . . ." He pointed at Fletcher and Felix, who were now clambering aboard St. John's dray. Suddenly Mark found himself looking down the barrels of a dozen pistols. "On the other hand, if you'd rather not. . . ." He shrugged and climbed into the back of the dray to pick up some of the coins I had dropped. "I'll just pay you now and we'll be on our way."

When he held out the glittering coins on his palm, the man in the sailor's cap just stared at them. "We agreed on a double eagle per man," Mark reminded him.

The man in the sailor's cap reached up with his free hand, grabbing hold of Mark's wrist and yanking Mark out of the wagon so that he fell headfirst through the air, spilling gold coins onto the street. Someone else shoved me from behind so that I landed right beside Mark.

By the time I sat up again, the man in the sailor's cap had taken over the dray's seat and started it off while the others began climbing over its sides and back. "Nice serving with you, Captain." The man in the sailor's cap gave Mark a mock salute.

"Consider yourself dishonorably discharged." Mark rose slowly and, as he dusted off his suit, watched his former army leave him. "I wonder how long it's going to take me to make up for that lost gold out of my salary?"

"Well," I said, "you owe money to almost everyone else. You might as well add Mr. Lincoln to the list."

Suddenly we were almost knocked over. The gunfire stopped, the curious had begun to appear on the street again; and, at the sight of the gold scattered in the dirt, people began scrambling and fighting with one another for the gold coins.

Helplessly Mark and I stepped to one side. The other intersection was clear now. "St. John's going to escape with the rest of his gold," I complained.

"Let's see what we can do about that." Mark started back for the Mint.

· CHAPTER ·
9

The door to the Mint had been left open. When Mark and I went inside, we discovered five soldiers, bound and gagged. They were lying on their sides trying to untie each other's hands, which had been placed behind them. When Mark undid the gag of the closest one, we found ourselves looking down at Corporal Malloy.

"I know you, don't I?" Malloy frowned up at Mark. "That's right. I saw you with the other reporters that day they found Johnny." Then he saw me and his eyes widened. "And the Duke. What are you two doing here?"

"Never mind that." Mark turned the corporal over onto his stomach to untie his hands. "What happened to you?"

Malloy twisted his head around. "It wasn't my fault. Felix Pettibone let those thieves in."

Mark went to the next man and began untying his hands. "How long have they been at this?"

Malloy began rubbing the circulation back into his wrists. "Just about the whole night. They've made over a dozen trips by now."

In the meantime, I had freed the hands of a third

soldier. "Do you remember which direction they usually went in?"

With stiff, clumsy fingers, Malloy began to untie his ankles. "I think the wagon went east."

"Then the major must be running for the ocean," I said to Mark.

"Must be." Mark glanced at the stand of rifles in one corner. "Want to get even with them?" he asked Malloy.

"I wouldn't mind repaying the little favor they did me," Malloy growled.

"Then let's go after them." Mark went on to the fourth man. "Just leave one man here to guard the Mint. I've sent someone to get the police. I just hope that Bulldog believes Harte."

When all the soldiers were untied, Mark and I set off with Malloy and three of his squad. We had to take it slow for the first block because the men were still a little wobbly on their legs; but by the second block they had begun to walk steadily and by the third we were taking it at the double-quick, moving straight down Commercial Street for the Long Wharf.

When we reached the waterfront, Mark stopped, looking first to the south and then to the north. In the distance, by the Pacific Street Wharf, he sighted what looked like a dray. "There," he pointed. We set off at a run again.

The draft horse looked familiar; but the wharf itself was empty except for an old man in a stained, ankle-length duster coat. He was sitting on the wharf, kicking his legs in the air as he fished. It was Beany, a hoppy, or opium addict, who lived around the wharf whenever he was out of money.

"Hey, Beany," I called and waved to him. "Did you see some soldiers get out of that dray and get on board a boat?"

Beany could be a nasty sort of person when he didn't have his pipeful. He turned his pinched, blood-shot eyes toward us.

Mark dug out a half dime. "Here."

Beany bit the coin and then his hand hid the coin away somewhere underneath his large coat. "They come rumbling up in that contraption and piled on board a tug." He pointed toward the head of the wharf. "They just left."

We walked all the way to the end of the Pacific Street Wharf. Putting a hand to his forehead to shade his eyes, Mark squinted toward the distance. Far away, like a fat drop of cream, a tugboat was making its way across the bay. "Too late," he muttered. Frustrated, he turned his back on the spectacle and caught sight of the *Rapidan*, which still lay at anchor at the Broadway Street Wharf right across from us.

"Come on." He caught me by the arm. "I promised to show you the ocean, didn't I?" Our feet pounded the boards as we sprinted back toward the dray, which the soldiers were inspecting. "This way, Sergeant," Mark called as we ran past.

"It's corporal," Malloy corrected him.

"You'll be a sergeant by the time I'm finished." Mark was already halfway to the hole at the foot of the Broadway Street Wharf.

Lieutenant Bainbridge himself was away from his tug, leaving only a cautious young ensign by the name of Purcell in charge of a crew much hung over from the night before. "I don't know," said the ensign, after listening to Mark's hurried explanation. "I think I ought to wait for orders from the lieutenant."

"By that time the raiders could have transferred the gold to a ship and be off any place. We've got to go after them now," Mark insisted.

"Listen to the man," Malloy warned. "If those raiders get away, you won't even get to command a rowboat."

Ensign Purcell glanced at Malloy and then back at Mark. "I can understand why the army's so anxious to take off after them, but why are you?" he asked Mark.

"I'm a reporter from the *Call.* The name's Mark Twain."

"Hey, you're the fellow who came by the other day." The ensign's face lit up instantly. "I didn't get a chance to tell you how much I've enjoyed your stories, sir." He took Mark's hand and began pumping it. "Reporters are a dime a dozen, but a humorous writer is hard to find."

Mark scratched the tip of his nose. "Well, it's true that there are an awful lot of writers in this city who make their jokes sound like sermons and their sermons like jokes." He arched his thick eyebrows. "Now if we might go after those Confederates? . . ."

The ensign paused and then nodded, his natural youthful enthusiasm finally taking control. "Yes, why not? The men could use a little exercise."

Leaving the ensign to rouse his crew, Mark made his way to the bow, trailed by a curious corporal and his squad of soldiers. "You are really Mr. Mark Twain?" the corporal asked eagerly.

"Well, y-a-a-s." Mark prepared himself for more compliments. "I have that dubious pleasure."

Malloy took off his cap and his fingers began to probe under the sweatband. "I was in this poker game a week ago and I won this note." He pulled out a much crumbled and folded IOU, which Mark had signed for twenty dollars about a year before. "I never thought I would find you so fast. This is really a stroke of luck."

"Quite so, Corporal. Quite so." Mark frowned at the note. "I must have signed it on that earlier visit to San Francisco." A sudden breeze appeared to snatch it out of his hand. "Oh, no." He seemed to make a grab for the note but actually blocked Corporal Malloy from reaching it. The two of them watched as the note fluttered into the sky out over the bay. "Of course I'll honor it," Mark assured the corporal, adding almost mechanically by now, "See me next Saturday. That's payday."

"I'll be there, *Mister* Mark Twain." Malloy sullenly pulled his cap over his eyes.

Then the *Rapidan* gave a shudder. There was a loud clonking sound from somewhere inside the tug, which settled down into a steady, pounding rhythm. I put my hand to the railing and felt the steady vibrations as the pistons began to move. The huge paddle wheels on the sides began to turn with loud splashing sounds and long plumes of white water went spreading across the water.

"Cast off the lines," Purcell called from the wheelhouse.

An old sailor appeared on the wharf near the *Rapidan*'s bow. He looked as if he had been gotten up hurriedly since he was only wearing a red union suit and a pair of bell-bottom trousers. He eased a heavy loop of cable from a wharf piling and threw it onto the deck with a thud. He followed a moment later. A pair of heavy shoes had been tied together and hung around his neck. He began to coil the cable neatly to the side. When he saw me staring, he winked but did not stop working. "Them shoes hurt my feet." He did a little dance on deck, and his bare feet slapped the boards harder than shoe leather. "Like to feel the ship under my feet."

"It's my first boat ride," I announced excitedly. "At least that I remember." I had come around the Horn when I was small, but I did not remember anything of the voyage.

"Is it now?" He fished a round, tan-colored biscuit from his pocket. "Then stick this hardtack in your belly." His palm cut a smooth path through the air. "I guarantee with that sitting like a stone in your stomach you won't feel sick at all."

As the tug began to turn its bow away from the wharf, I cautiously tapped the hardtack on the railing. The hardtack was as solid as a rock. "How do you eat it? Swallow it?"

The old sailor slipped another hardtack from his pocket. "You put it in your mouth and you suck on it and then swallow each little layer as it crumbles." He opened his mouth, revealing only four teeth that I could see, and popped the hardtack into his mouth.

When we neared the head of the wharf, I could feel the deck shiver and the sidewheels begin to turn faster, sending up a fine spray over the sides. We were gathering speed.

The old sailor took his own hardtack from his mouth. "Hey, better get away from the bow," he warned Mark and the soldiers.

Mark was at the very front of the bow with his legs

spread for balance and one hand holding onto the railing. "Don't worry about me," Mark turned to say, "I'm an old sailor."

But there was a strong wind blowing that day, and as the tug emerged into the choppy bay waters, the bow dipped suddenly in a trough between waves. A huge sheet of salty spray drenched Mark and the others.

"Can't tell a landlubber anything." The sailor popped his hardtack back into his mouth.

"Get those guns out of this spray." Mark frantically waved the soldiers away from the bow even as another sheet of spray splashed over them.

The wet, dripping soldiers walked in single file to the small cabin behind and a little beneath the wheelhouse. Mark was the last. As he passed, he stared at me. "What have you got inside your mouth? Your cheeks are bulging like a stuffed chipmunk's."

I didn't answer as I followed Mark into the cabin. Bunks filled three walls. A kerosene lantern swinging from the ceiling gave some light. Soldiers sat on the lower bunks and on the floor inspecting the percussion locks of their rifles. Anxiously Mark stood swaying in the doorway as the tug began to chug its way northward. Through the portholes I could see San Francisco slide by.

"What's the verdict?" Mark finally asked.

"Most of the percussion caps and almost all the cartridges are wet." Malloy raised his rifle fatalistically. "I'm afraid this gun is all we've got left."

A worried Mark backed out of the doorway, bumping into me. He did not even glance at me but made his way back along the side and up the ladder to the wheelhouse.

I wanted to stay outside, though, and enjoy my ride; but my eyes happened to look back toward Telegraph Hill where Johnny Dougherty had died.

I hadn't really thought about Johnny in all this time—maybe because I'd shut him out of my life so often before this. I wasn't exactly *glad* that Johnny Dougherty was dead, but I wasn't exactly sad either. In fact, I had half expected Johnny to come back from the dead out of sheer meanness and spite. After all, he was of more use to the Devil up here than down below.

We were just passing Alcatraz Island with its tall lighthouse and all its bristling cannon when I saw the birds slipping light and easy over the waves. I had seen one or two of them sitting on wharf pilings before this. They were mostly black with long, drawn-out necks like someone had tried to stretch out a duck by dragging it through a sooty chimney. They were so ugly that I used to chuck rocks at them.

But seeing them out on the water was something else. There were about a dozen of them, flying one behind the other so that they looked like black beads hanging on an invisible string that was being jerked up and down. They liked to hug the surface of the water, I suppose, so they could see the fish, and as the water would suddenly rise in a swell, they would dart upward—still in line.

They swept low over the water, necks arched like arrows, their black oval backs round and smooth as wet, polished stones. Sometimes their wing tips even brushed the water with quick, wet slaps as they skimmed the tops of the waves—as if they were playing a game of tag with the water. I was surprised at how graceful they were and a little ashamed because I had only thought they were good as targets for my rock throwing.

I suppose most anything will look ugly away from its proper place—even a lazy, cowardly reporter like Mark, or a young lord like myself—even Johnny Dougherty. I guess there must have been some good in Johnny Dougherty or my mother would never have married him. It was just that by the time I grew old enough to be aware of things, the good in Johnny had been buried a long time.

For the first time in my life, I wondered what had made Johnny go bad like that—only there wasn't anyone who could tell me. It was sad the way things worked out sometimes, and no one to make them better. I began to shiver, so I wrapped my arms around myself and ran my hands up and down my sides. Though the city was warm, the air was cold out on the bay and the sharp winds made it seem even colder. But it wasn't just my outside that was cold; it was my inside, too, with all of these sad and lonely thoughts whirling around my mind.

Suddenly I did not want to be by myself, so I climbed up to the wheelhouse where I knew it would be warm and dry and where Mark would be.

Ensign Purcell was at the wheel while Mark stood to the right. Mark had a collapsible brass telescope in his hand, which he was aiming in the direction the ensign was pointing. "They're already near the Golden Gate," he instructed Mark. "Can you see them?"

Mark fooled around with the sections of the telescope until he had it in focus. "Y-a-a-s, I can see a tug with little blue-uniformed figures. Buy why is it running so slowly?"

The ensign held the spokes of the wheel, shifting it

slightly every now and then. "The closer you get to the bar at the mouth of the Golden Gate," he explained, "the stronger the currents get. I'll bet they're straining the boilers in that old tug just to make *that* speed."

"And we have to go through that, too." Mark lowered the telescope glumly.

"But the *Rap* is newer and bigger." The ensign patted the wheel affectionately. "I'll bet you my next month's salary that we'll catch up with them by the time we get to the Golden Gate."

"It's a bet I'd be happy to lose." Mark played nervously with the telescope. "But I'm afraid that my salary is already much abused."

There was a tall stool at the back of the wheelhouse, and I sat on it while I looked through the windows. To my right lay the tall peak of Mount Tamalpais above the rolling hills of Marin, while to my left and just a little ahead of us was the solid brick bulk of San Francisco's Fort Point.

I took the hardtack from my mouth. "Say, can't you signal to the fort with flags? Maybe they could put a warning shot across the major's bow."

The ensign glanced back at me. "Who's that?"

"His Grace, the Duke of Baywater." Mark raised and lowered the sections of the telescope. "What do you think about his suggestion?"

"I guess we could signal the fort; but," the ensign wondered, "do you want to risk sinking the boat?"

Mark jammed the telescope sections together. "No, and the men on the boat know that. They wouldn't turn back."

I got down from the stool. The hardtack tasted like

old paste to me. Opening the wheelhouse door slightly I threw the hardtack out into the sea. I just hoped there wasn't a stray fish right underneath or it would crack that poor fish's skull.

The minutes ticked away on the clock in the wheelhouse. Mark kept checking every few moments with the telescope. "You know," he said finally, his eye tightly screwed to the telescope, "I do believe you're right, Ensign. I'd say we've gained a half mile on them."

The ensign stroked one of the wheel spokes. "I'd match the *Rap* against any tug any day."

Mark laid the telescope down on a small shelf to the side. "What about letting them know we're coming? Let's send a friendly little bullet at them."

"It might distract them in the wheelhouse," the ensign agreed. "Why not?"

Mark started for the door, but I was already out of it and down the ladder. I raced along the deck to the door to the cabin. "Corporal," I panted, "you're wanted on deck."

Malloy rose slowly. I wouldn't say that he and his squad were sick, but they did not look all that good. I suppose it was not the easiest thing to be tied up all night and then be taken for a boat ride on a choppy bay. His rifle had been wrapped in a piece of oilcloth borrowed, I suppose, from one of the sailors. Carrying his precious gun, he made his way over the legs and bodies of his squad to the cabin door. "Have we caught them yet?"

"No, but we nearly have," I said, trying to think positively.

Mark was waiting by the ladder to the wheelhouse. He had left his hat inside the wheelhouse so that the wind was blowing his hair all around his head. He had tried turning up his collar against the spray but that did not do much good, it seemed to me. All of us looked like soaked rats.

Mark waved to Malloy and shouted to make his voice heard above the wind. "Do you think you can get off a shot in this spray?"

Malloy looked around, blinking his eyes against the fine mist that seemed to hover in the air. It was not actually foggy, but the side wheels churned up a steady drizzle that hovered over the boat. "I can try," Malloy finally said. With one hand on the side of the cabin and the other holding his rifle, he cautiously began to follow Mark to the bow.

The ship ahead of us wallowed like a fat seagull. Beyond the Golden Gate, the blue ocean waters spread like a giant, empty tray. Once they were out on that, it seemed to me, they could lose themselves forever.

Malloy had spread his legs, trying to get his balance on the rocking boat; but he was having trouble. Mark braced his legs against the base of the wheelhouse and put his hands to Malloy's waist. He nodded for me to copy him.

When Malloy felt himself steadied by two pairs of hands, he began to unwrap his gun. A sudden dip of the bow sent a sheet of spray over us. "I don't know if the gun will stay dry enough." He had to shout to make himself heard as he blinked and wiped at his eyes.

Mark licked the salt spray from his lips. "I still think we ought to send them a little greeting."

Malloy waited, timing it for when the bow suddenly lifted. Quickly he whipped the oilcloth away from his gun, brought the gun butt up to his shoulder, and aimed. The ship pitched suddenly to the left. He swore grimly and reaimed. His finger twitched at the trigger. Since we were right behind him, the explosion of his shot was almost deafening.

"They're ducking for cover," Purcell announced to us from the wheelhouse. He must have been checking on things with his telescope.

Malloy hurriedly sidestepped around Mark and went back inside the cabin to reload where it was dry. The spray was even heavier and the movement of the ship in the choppy water more violent by the time he reappeared on the deck.

"This shot . . . I don't know. . . ." Malloy shook his head, his hair flying back from his ears.

"Let's see, anyway." Mark urged him. We planted our feet against the wheelhouse again and gripped Malloy's waist to steady him. Malloy spread his legs a little further apart for better balance. Taking a deep breath, he raised his rifle and began to take painstaking aim; but before he could fire, we heard a muffled roar.

Mark looked up in surprise. Out in the Golden Gate, an orange-red ball of fire was sending off sooty-gray plumes of smoke. The old tug had exploded, sending a fortune in gold to the bottom of the bay.

·CHAPTER·
10

Bulldog was waiting for us when we returned to the Broadway Street Wharf. With him was a much humbler Captain Purdy and a squad of soldiers.

Mark stood at the bow as the sailors moored the tug to its berth. "Where's Harte?"

"At the Mint waiting for the treasurer and the superintendent." Bulldog pointed impatiently toward the bay. "What happened out there?"

"Their boat exploded, Bulldog. The boilers probably overheated." Mark spread his hands helplessly. "We could only recover five bodies: the tug's captain, a crewman, two fellows in soldiers' uniforms and Pettibone. There wasn't any sign of Fletcher and St. John, but the ensign says the currents could have carried their bodies anywhere. As for the gold, well, it would take Neptune to get it back now."

"We're collecting the gold you spread around Pacific Street." Bulldog nodded behind him. "Why did you have to wait for my day off to start all this ruckus?"

Mark climbed onto the wharf. "I did try to warn you earlier."

Bulldog cleared his throat. "Yes, I guess you did. You

want me to apologize to you now or over dinner?"

"I'll take one now and one later, Bulldog."

"And I apologize, too," Captain Purdy said gloomily. I suppose he had just realized that his career had probably sunk along with the gold. "I wish I'd listened to you," he added significantly, "*Mister* Twain."

"Don't you think you owe an apology to His Grace as well?" Mark motioned to me.

Bulldog touched the brim of his hat, while the captain nodded his head.

Satisfied, Mark scratched his unshaven chin. "That Confederate major was out to do more than steal our gold, you know: He was going to discredit President Lincoln." Mark's finger traced an imaginary sentence from a newspaper editorial. "A fortune in gold was snatched today from the hands of an incompetent government to let the Confederates prolong the war." Mark shook his head. "I suppose folks might have gotten disgusted enough to vote Mr. Lincoln out and the Peace Democrats in."

"Oh, my God." A very pale Captain Purdy took out his handkerchief and mopped his forehead. "They just might have."

"Come on. All this talk of politics makes me thirsty." Bulldog rubbed his throat for emphasis.

Mark glanced over his shoulder at the bay. "I can't, just yet. I'm not sure what ship they were on and I need that for my story."

He turned and caught sight of Beany, who was still fishing from the Pacific Street Wharf. "I'll just check with that old fellow and see if he knows."

We walked quickly around from the Broadway Street

Wharf to the other. "Say, oldtimer," Mark said to Beany, "what was the name of the tug the soldiers were on?"

Beany simply hawked and spat. Mark hunted in his pocket and found another half dime to give to him.

Beany tested it with his teeth and then stowed the coin away. "Why?"

"Because it blew up," Mark snapped.

"Did it now?" the old wharf rat lowered his fishing pole, suddenly interested. "Well, she was the *Klamath Bay*."

Mark made a dutiful note of the fact. "Do you happen to. . . ."

Beany simply held out his dirty palm.

Mark dug out a dime this time to give him. "This ought to be good for two questions, right?"

"Yup." Beany blinked his eyes and paused for a moment. "Now what's your second question?"

"Why, you larcenous old man." Mark started to boil.

Bulldog cleared his throat. "This isn't getting us any faster to a restaurant."

"All right." Mark glared at Beany. "Would you happen to know any names of the crew?"

"Let's see. Hollins was the captain and Jimmy was his mate." Beany held up one foot to study his broken shoe. "But I didn't know those four soldiers."

"You mean five, don't you?" Mark demanded.

Beany simply eyed Mark.

Mark waved at him impatiently. "You'll get paid."

Beany shrugged. "I can count. There weren't but four who went past me."

"Bulldog, give this fellow a half eagle, will you?" Mark

patted the detective's arm. He left the indignant Brill before the angry detective could protest and took Captain Purdy by the arm. "Come on, Captain. It looks like the chase is still on. We'd better get Malloy and his boys."

As they walked back toward the *Rapidan* to fetch Malloy and his squad, Mark began excitedly to explain to the captain. "That Confederate major must have set up the *Klamath Bay* as a decoy in case he was pursued."

I chimed in. "I'll bet he had a bomb planted on board—only the others didn't know about it. When they reached the Golden Gate, Fletcher or the major lit the fuse and got over the side. If we didn't find the body, we'd just think it'd been washed out to sea."

"Then we've got a whole city to search." The captain surveyed the skyline uncomfortably.

"Maybe not." Mark slowed thoughtfully. "How much did they get?"

"It's only an estimate, but it's something like half a million dollars." The captain buttoned up his coat. "They'll have to have a full accounting at the Mint."

"That's a powerful lot of gold to haul," Mark mused to himself. He eyed the nearby warehouses. "Or to store away." Mark quickened his stride. "Corporal Malloy said that the drays were always heading for the waterfront. My guess is that a ship with the gold is probably at some wharf south of here with Fletcher on board. If you begin searching down there, I'll get the ensign to take me out so we can cut off any ships trying to leave."

It took the ensign some five minutes to get up steam again. Malloy and his men were still on board, since they had been helping to remove the corpses recovered from the Golden Gate. The lines were just being cast off when Bulldog, with a running jump, managed to make the deck of the tug.

Mark helped to steady the detective. "Nothing like a Sunday of salt air and exercise, is there, Bulldog?"

Bulldog put his hands against the cabin. "Nothing like a nosy reporter, you mean. You're pretty lavish with my money."

"You ought to see how I just spent the U.S. government's." Mark pantomimed the scattering of coins. "Gold coins flung all over the street. Just like a French king." He added as an afterthought, "Or an American congressman." Eagerly Mark climbed up to the wheelhouse. Ensign Purcell was standing before the wheel again.

His eyes on the bay, the ensign nodded his head when he heard us enter. "Do you reporters always have such exciting times?"

Mark picked up a half-full mug of coffee from on top of a stool and began to sip from it. "What do you mean, Ensign?" Mark asked innocently. "Sundays are always my slow days." With the telescope in one hand, he began scanning the bay.

"Where to? Along the coast line?" the ensign asked.

"Wait a moment." Mark hastily set the mug down on a stool. He aimed the telescope toward the faintest white streak to the north. It must have been the trail of a ship. "Y-a-a-s, well, what do you know." Mark held the telescope for me to look through. "See anyone familiar?"

I could make out a small steam tug with its gunwales riding very low in the water as if it carried a heavy cargo. There, on the deck, glancing at his watch, was Fletcher in a black broadcloth frock coat.

"They're moving so slow." I stood back from the telescope.

Mark collapsed the telescope sections together with a click. "They're probably heavily loaded; and anyway, Fletcher doesn't have any reason to think that our ship is after him."

"Full steam ahead?" The ensign excitedly adjusted his grips on the spokes of the wheel.

"Better just speed up a little." Mark rubbed his chin. "Enough to shorten the distance between us but not enough to frighten Fletcher."

Leaving the wheelhouse, we went back to warn the others in the cabin that we had sighted Fletcher and to stay hidden until Mark sent word.

"I hope it's a short trip," Bulldog muttered miserably from his chair. "I've never felt sicker in my life and I've got you to thank for this."

"If you'd listened to me earlier, we wouldn't be out here," Mark couldn't resist saying.

Bulldog closed his eyes. "You can write whatever you like about this caper, but if you write one word about my being seasick"—he jabbed a finger blindly at Mark—"I'll put you away for a hundred years."

Mark jammed his hands into his pockets and leaned against the cabin wall with a great air of satisfaction. "Seeing you suffer is payment enough."

"One thing, Mr. Twain." Malloy waved a hand at his squad. "Mine is still the only gun that works."

The smile faded from Mark's face. "You'd better make every shot count, then."

As we left the cabin and made our way back to the

wheelhouse, we could see Fletcher's tug more clearly now. It had reached the end of the San Francisco peninsula and had begun to angle not due west toward the ocean but northwest toward the Marin peninsula. Casually, almost insolently, Fletcher's tug took its time passing by the army guns on Alcatraz Island which lay to its left. You would almost have thought Fletcher was sightseeing.

Mark gripped the railing to keep his balance. "He's got his nerve, all right." He shook his head in admiration.

The ensign glanced over his shoulder at us when we entered the wheelhouse. "If the tug keeps this course, she'll tie up at Sausalito."

"Where's that?" I asked.

"It's a small town on the eastern side of the Marin peninsula." Mark picked up the telescope and handed it to me. "Look for it in the willow trees."

At the foot of the hills that covered the Marin peninsula, I could make out small shacks. Willow trees with long, graceful, hairlike branches grew all around there. Sausalito stood near the mouth to Richardson's Bay, which, Mark explained, was formed on the west and north by the bulk of the Marin peninsula and a smaller offshoot of land called the Belvedere peninsula, which was covered on one side with thick, gnarly oaks.

Off the tip of the Belvedere peninsula sat a small island the color and shape of a piece of taffy melting in the sun. Camp Reynolds was the fancy title given to the battery of guns that sat behind a set of dirt walls. The soldiers were busy adding to the battery's protection. Fletcher's tug not only passed near the island, but Fletcher himself waved to the soldiers and they waved back as he entered Richardson's Bay.

Mark made me lower the telescope. "Better warn the others to be ready to come on deck when we call."

"All right." Handing the telescope to Mark, I carried the message to the cabin. When I returned to the wheelhouse, I found Mark explaining the situation to the ensign, who did not look at all happy.

"You mean they had a bomb on board that other ship?" His knuckles were white as they curled around the wheel spokes. "We could have been blown to bits, too." His eyes were fixed on Fletcher's tug as it put into the slips at Sausalito, and the young ensign looked as if he wished the *Rapidan* were miles away.

Fletcher stood in the stern, his arms folded, taking in the scene. The hills stretched like arms enclosing calm waters. Small boats rode at the Sausalito slips; and beyond, near the top of the bay, were marshlands where birds circled.

We were twenty feet away when Fletcher began scratching the back of his neck as if he could feel our eyes watching him. Maybe it was his days as a bush-whacker that made him suspect ambushes. Or maybe he was simply nervous. But he turned at that moment to look at our tug. He stared right at the *Rapidan*'s wheelhouse and his mouth dropped open when he saw us; but he did not stay surprised for more than an instant before he turned. Fletcher began waving his arms frantically at his crew and dimly we could hear him shouting to cast off the lines. Then he dashed inside the wheelhouse of his tug.

I stuck my head outside. "He's seen us," I shouted.

The cabin door burst open and Malloy went racing to the bow with his rifle clutched in his hand. A rather unsteady Bulldog followed him.

Mark turned to the ensign. "Can you put us alongside?"

The ensign licked his lips. "But how do you know he doesn't have a bomb on board that boat, too?" Now that he was facing what was probably his first test of fire, the ensign seemed to be having second thoughts.

"Even if he does," Mark snapped, "it's a mighty short swim to shore."

The ensign shook his head. "No, I don't dare go any nearer."

"I'm not giving up now—not when we're this close." Mark grasped both arms of the startled young ensign and spun him away so that the ensign and I fell together into a corner. He bagan to shout directions through the tube for the engine room to cut our speed. Outside, I heard the crack of a rifle shot.

"Mr. Twain, this is a navy boat." The ensign managed to untangle himself and tried to pull Mark away from the wheel; but Mark's grip was unbreakable.

"Then I'm joining temporarily," Mark grunted.

I got hold of the brass telescope then and brought it down over the ensign's head. "I hope his skull's thick enough," I said, as I watched the young ensign slump to the floor. Just to make sure, I knelt to feel the pulse at his neck. He seemed all right.

"You know," Mark observed to me, "you're getting right handy to have around."

When I got to my feet again, Mark was easing the *Rapidan* in toward the other tug. Malloy was in the bow frantically reloading his rifle while the rest of his squad brandished their own useless guns. Bulldog lay on his hands and knees on the starboard side.

With one hand on a wheel spoke, Mark stretched as far as he could to jerk open the door to the wheelhouse. Gathering as much air as he could into his lungs, he shouted over to the other tug, "Better come out on deck with your hands up." His voice managed to carry through the still air.

The captain of the other tug climbed down from the wheelhouse staring up at the bullet hole in the window. The other sailors had gathered at the stern with their hands in the air.

The *Rapidan* was about five feet away from the stern of the other ship when Fletcher appeared. He had a large dark brown bottle in his hand. "Stand off," he shrilled. "I've got Greek fire in this bottle.† I'll send your whole boat up in flames."

Mark had already cut off the engines as we glided in slowly toward the other tug. On the bow, Malloy turned indecisively to look up at Mark. From the grim expression on Fletcher's face, it was more than likely he did have something in that bottle.

Suddenly we heard a pistol shot. Fletcher clutched at his shoulder, the bottle falling from his hand over the side and landing with a loud splash in the water. I glanced down at the starboard side and saw Bulldog

---

†Greek fire was a name given to different liquids created to cause fires which would be difficult to put out with water. The idea is first credited to the Byzantine Greeks who used it as a secret weapon in A.D. 673.

calmly lowering his smoking pistol. The only cure Bulldog Brill needed for his seasickness was to see his quarry.

A few minutes later, Mark and I entered the cabin of the other tug. Fletcher lay sprawled across several layers of sacks, staring at us sullenly. "I knew we should have killed you two right away." He gave a grunt. "It was you who sicced them on us, wasn't it?"

With a borrowed pocketknife, Mark cut open Fletcher's broadcloth coat and shirt to expose his shoulder. "We just asked ourselves what a bushwhacker was likely to do."

"Well, if I had to be outsmarted, at least it was by a Missourian." Fletcher watched calmly as Mark tore open his shirt.

"Bulldog has made a real mess of your shoulder." Mark took out the bottle of whisky that Bulldog had found on board the *Rapidan* and began to douse the wound.

"I seen worse." Fletcher winced and took his breath in sharply.

"We'll stop the bleeding, anyway, until a doctor can take out the ball." Mark corked the bottle and lodged it securely between two coin sacks.

Fletcher smiled grimly. "Going to save me for the noose?" He nodded to his soldier's coat and pants. "They hang spies, you know."

"So I hear." Mark waved me over. "All right, Your Grace. You can bandage him now."

Bulldog had instructed me to let Mark do all the talking because he wanted to see what Mark could find out. He figured Fletcher might clam up if anyone else tried to talk with the raider. I just concentrated on winding the bandage over Fletcher's shoulder, under his armpit, and back over his shoulder again.

Fletcher shook his head grimly. "You wouldn't have been on our trail so fast if Johnny hadn't gotten greedy."

"You mean the penny?" Mark asked.

"Yeah." Fletcher eyed me. "When Felix saw you pick up that coin, he figured it must have rolled out of Johnny's pocket during the fight with Gogarty." Fletcher inspected my handiwork. "Did you fellows get up that bottle of Greek fire?"

"No." Mark settled down on the sacks of coins. "We figure it landed in the mud. I don't know if we can ever bring it up."

"Well, I wish you would move the boat then." Fletcher rubbed his thumb along his lower lip. "Still, I'm not sure it's all that dangerous with a whole ocean on top of it. The major was the one who brewed that particular bottle." He nodded to Mark. "Speaking of the Devil, what happened to the major and the boys?"

"The boys are dead." Mark rearranged the heavy sacks so that there was some support for his back. "The ship exploded right in the middle of the Golden Gate. We recovered all of the bodies except the major's."

Gently I made a lengthwise tear in the bandage and wound the two halves around the shoulder before I tied them into a knot.

"If you ask me," Mark said, "it's pretty suspicious. I think there was a bomb on board."

Apparently Fletcher was of the same mind. "That cold-blooded sidewinder," Fletcher said softly. "It'd be just like him to do that." Fletcher let his head sink back against the coins. "He told me they were just going to put him off near the shore and then lead you a merry chase out to sea. There was supposed to be a horse and warm clothing near the beach. Then he'd ride to Sausalito and we'd go to some bay up the northern coast and transfer the cargo to a ship that would take it to Canada."

"And you would have had a solid gold embarrassment for Mr. Lincoln." Mark held out a cigarette he had made himself with tobacco and paper borrowed from a sailor. "Have a smoke?"

"Much obliged." Fletcher took it and tried to lean back against several sacks of coins. "You'd think a bed as expensive as this would be more comfortable." He squirmed uneasily. "We were supposed to meet right about now."

Mark took a match from his pocket. "That major is . . . or was . . . a clever man."

"Too clever." Fletcher lolled his head on the coin sacks. "It'd be just like him to cover his tracks by blowing up the ship."

Mark struck the match against his shoe sole. "That's the troubled with this war; it got taken over by the Major St. Johns of this country. You don't just beat the enemy. You burn down all the farms and drive off all the livestock."

Fletcher fingered the cigarette thoughtfully. "The major used to like to quote a fellow called Tacitus: 'They make a desolation and call it peace.'"

Mark sighed, "Y-a-a-s, well, the major's at peace now, anyway. The water's mighty cold even in the summer."

At first, I thought Fletcher was staring at Mark. Then I

realized that Fletcher was staring instead at the fiery-headed match.

Suddenly Fletcher let his breath out in a rush. "Mister, don't you ever underestimate the major. All them mild manners and talk, well, they ain't nothing more than a shell—a husk from his old life that the major still wears like a snake stuck in his old skin." He took hold of Mark's wrist and pulled the match down to the tip of his cigarette. When it was lit, he let go of Mark's arm and took a long, steady pull before he took the cigarette from his lips to puff out a long, thin streamer of smoke. "The major's a shark. A human shark. It's going to take more than an ocean to kill him."

· CHAPTER ·

11

While the ensign returned to San Francisco to take the news to Captain Purdy, Mark and I went out with Bulldog and some of the other soldiers to patrol the roads into Sausalito while Malloy kept a watch on Fletcher and the others. We tramped around for maybe an hour before Captain Purdy came tearing along with a platoon of soldiers.

From the way he carried on, you would have thought someone had set fire to his pants. He requisitioned every horse from a stable, though the stable owner was almost in tears because some of the horses had either been promised to his regular customers or because some of the horses were simply being boarded there. But the captain went ahead anyway and made cavalrymen out of two squads of soldiers, though most of them looked as if they were lucky to know which was the front end of the horse. He sent those men off to cover the different beaches around Marin.

In the meantime, the captain kept shuttling men over from Camp Reynolds until he had every road into Sausalito sealed off. After another hour of marching, Mark and I decided that we had had enough of the army.

From a nearby house on the edge of town, Mark borrowed—or "requisitioned," if you like—about a dozen sheets of paper and three pencils.

"Aren't you going to patrol any more?" Bulldog wanted to know.

"Trying to catch the major with this clumsy-footed horde is like trying to catch a mosquito with a fish net." Mark pointed to a spot shaded by several willow trees which grew by the main road into town. "I am going to make history right there."

We sat down with our backs against the trunk of one tree. Mark handed me his penknife—he had bought it from the sailor who had originally only planned to lend it to him—with instructions to keep the points sharp. "If this story doesn't make me known back in the States, then nothing will."

"States?" I frowned, puzzled.

"Back east." Mark began to write hurriedly. He was still at it an hour later when Captain Purdy and a sour-looking Bulldog came striding up to us.

"Any luck, Captain?" Mark did not even look up as he crossed out an entire paragraph.

"I'm afraid not, Mr. Twain."

"Well, no matter. I can go to press with what's happening up to now." Mark began writing his paragraph over again.

"Sorry,"—Captain Purdy had the secure, confident smile of a man with four aces and a fifth up his sleeve—"but you can't print this story."

Mark went on writing stubbornly. "This is too big a story to cover up. You're sending soldiers all over Marin."

"Maneuvers." Captain Purdy's lips played with each syllable of the word as if he knew it would answer almost any question. He had managed to salvage his career after all, perhaps at the cost of Mark's. "Mr. Twain," he explained in a sweet, calm voice as if to a small, rather spoiled child, "the truth about what happened today could embarrass President Lincoln almost as much as a successful theft would have done. The way things are now, he's going to have a hard enough time without giving more ammunition to his opponents."

With his dreams collapsing around him, Mark desperately lurched to his feet. "Captain, for the last three days I have been hounded, clubbed, and threatened; and whenever I tried to warn people like you, I was simply laughed at." He finished with a quiet dignity. "No one has the right to take this story away from me."

"I'd hate to have people laugh at you for trying to start another hoax." Obviously enjoying his position of power, the captain folded his arms like some indulgent parent trying to appear stern. "Worse, I'd hate to have to prosecute you for inciting a riot by trying to misrepresent what were only simple 'military maneuvers.'"

"Bulldog here will back me up." Mark gripped his friend's shoulder.

However, Bulldog would only look sideways at Mark. "I'm a Union man first." He shrugged off Mark's hand. "The captain's right about the story."

"Don't do this to me, Bulldog." Mark leaned forward to catch his friend's eyes in his; but Bulldog turned toward the houses of Sausalito. "I would have sworn you were the one honest man left in San Francisco." Mark's voice tightened. "And here you are helping Purdy to lie."

"Grow up, Mark," Bulldog snapped. "Sometimes there are more important things than the truth. We have to preserve the Union. Otherwise, all the suffering, all the tears, all the bloodshed—it won't mean one damn thing."

"If you say so, Bulldog." Mark slipped his pencil into his pocket. He stared up at the self-satisfied captain. "But you're going to give me at least this much: You're not going to hang Fletcher."

The captain tucked a thumb inside his belt. "He's a spy."

Mark folded the sheets of his story in half. "But you said yourself that there was no conspiracy—only certain 'military maneuvers.'"

The captain crisscrossed his arms several times in front of himself. "No, you're going too far, Mr. Twain. I'm not going to help the likes of Fletcher."

Mark regarded the captain calmly. "I don't think you realize just how far I'm prepared to go. If I go down, Captain," Mark warned quietly, "I'll do my darnedest to take you with me. At the very least, I'll cast enough doubt on your reputation so that you'll never get another promotion." Mark added, "Ask that sister in Nevada about my feud with the other newspaper writers. I can wield a pen dipped in venom and gunpowder."

Bulldog studied his nails. "If you are an ambitious man, Captain—and I believe you are—think twice about what Mark is saying. Some of those boys from Missouri can get downright suicidal when they get caught up in a feud. They don't care much what happens to them as long as they can get their enemies."

Captain Purdy swore softly under his breath in a

rather unimaginative and colorless way; I had expected more of New York profanity. "All right, I'll see that Fletcher gets a light sentence. He ought to be out of prison by the time the war is over."

"Your promise hardly inspires my trust," Mark said slowly.

"That's all I'm willing to do, Mr. Twain." The captain tipped his hat to Mark. "You'll have to be satisfied with that."

As an old bargainer, I recognized the tone of a man who had made his final offer. I glanced at Mark. He had realized the same thing. "Well, I suppose politics is the art of learning to live with frustration." Slipping his unfinished article into his pocket, Mark shook hands with the captain solemnly. "If you don't need us for anything, I'd like to go back to the city."

"Don't you want to be around when they bring in the major?" Bulldog asked.

Mark eyed the hills around us. "Somehow I've got this feeling in my bones that the major is long gone by now; but even if you did catch him," Mark shrugged, "you wouldn't let me write about it anyway."

"I suppose a lift back home is the least I owe you." Captain Purdy pointed toward the slips. "You can have the *Rapidan*."

Bulldog stood with his legs spread. "For what it's worth, Mark, I take back whatever I said before. You're a fine reporter."

"Well," Mark smiled tiredly, "I'm getting there."

When we returned to San Francisco, we found the waterfront as busy as usual. Drays and wagons rumbled by. Hacks rattled along carrying passengers to or from the ships. A concertina played a lively enough tune from a nearby ship. I lifted my head. This was the waterfront that I knew. I sniffed the air playfully. "I guess it's time to go off and see what kind of money I can make."

"I guess it is," Mark agreed, and stretched out his hand to me. "I can't say it's been a pleasure working with you; but it certainly hasn't been dull."

"If I hear of any good stories, I'll let you know." I took his hand and shook it. "Maybe they'll even let you publish it next time."

"Maybe." Mark grinned crookedly. "But the way my luck seems to go, I wouldn't count on it."

I let go of his hand, but I found it hard to walk away. "Well, I'll see you around."

"Right, Your Grace."

Funny, I'd only been with him a little over two days and yet I felt like I'd known him for most of my life. Maybe it was because we fit comfortably together now, like a hand into an old favorite glove. Or maybe it was because the Mark Twain I knew now was a little surer and a little more dedicated than the Mark I had first met. Or maybe it was just that I had learned to like him— despite all his faults.

And I guess Mark felt that way, too, because he called to me, "Hey, Baywater." He jingled the coins in his pants. "My money's burning an awful big hole in my pocket. Want to help me spend it at the Willows?"

I had heard a lot about the Willows but I had never actually gone there—though I had always wanted to go. The Willows was a large private park with small hills and meadows, which sounded pretty nice; but what I really wanted to see was the zoo with all the birds and animals, including a pond for sea lions.

Even so, I did my best to control my excitement. I stuffed my hands into my pockets and pretended to consider the matter. "Well, I guess I don't have anything better to do. But," I warned Mark, "I want to pay my own way in."

"Why not let me treat you?" He sounded hurt.

"I don't like owing people," I tried to explain.

"Y-a-a-s, well, there's a lot of folks in San Francisco who wouldn't think my hide was worth saving." Mark tucked his thumbs under his coat lapels. "However, I beg to differ with them. Treating you to the Willows is the least I can do for you."

Suspicious, I cocked my head to one side, trying to figure out Mark's angle, only I couldn't. Mark seemed to be making a sincere offer.

He lifted his hand toward me. "You know, sometimes it takes as much grace to accept a gift as it does to give one."

"All right," I shrugged. "I guess it's up to you if you want to throw your money away." I couldn't help smiling, though.

We were near one end of the North Beach and Mission streetcar line so we did not have any trouble getting seats, though as the streetcar rumbled along behind the plodding horses more and more couples and families began to squeeze their way on, some of them with large picnic hampers. By the time the streetcar covered the two miles to the Willows, it was jammed.

After buying the admission tickets, Mark got two mugs of lemonade from the restaurant. I would have preferred beer and said so, but Mark said I was too young. Taking a side path, we headed for the heart of the park: a hollow where a cool bubbling stream ran between banks lined with shady trees. We were lucky enough to find a spot in the shadow of a particularly large willow.

I rubbed at my nose as I sat down. "What's that stuffy, sweet smell?"

Mark laughed as he made a pillow of his coat. "I'm glad to see that there's something you don't know." He lay down carefully, trying to keep his mug upright. "It's fresh air you're smelling and trees growing and the rich, brown earth." He drank some of his lemonade. "And you're listening to the sound of the breeze through the willow trees and the quick, liquid music of the stream."

"I don't know that I like it all that much," I grumbled.

"No one died of a little nature." Mark laid his head down.

"Lightning's part of nature, isn't it?" Sipping my lemonade, I watched the families picnicking at the tables under the trees. Young men flirted with young women over on the dance platforms whenever the bands paused for a rest. It was like looking at a foreign country.

Then I heard a tooting kind of music. "What's that?"

"A calliope." Mark waved a hand vaguely in the air. "There's a merry-go-round around here someplace."

I swung my foot back and forth in time to the merry-go-round's music. "Maybe I'll try a ride on it—though I expect it'll be pretty tame compared to our ride from the Mint."

When Mark did not answer, I looked down at him. His eyes were shut tight and his mouth was opening in a snore. I grabbed his glass before it dropped from his fingers and set it down near his head.

I suppose not many folks work their way from the very bottom of their profession almost to the top in just two days and then find themselves at the very bottom again. He had earned his rest.

AFTERWORD

While there was never a Confederate raid on the Mint, there was a band of robbers operating in California that summer who claimed to be Confederate raiders. Moreover, the *Chapman* and *Haze* incidents actually happened; and the newspapers that year were full of other rumored raids. In fact, a Confederate privateer, the C.S.S. *Shenandoah*, cancelled its attack on San Francisco only when it discovered that the war had ended.

For the general atmosphere of the time, I would refer the reader to Edgar Branch's *Clemens of the Call*—to which this novel is heavily indebted. I would also like to express my gratitude to the San Francisco and Santa Clara libraries for their assistance, and a special word of thanks to the Sunnyvale librarians who have been so helpful in obtaining books and information for me.